Pascal Roussel

DIVINA INSIDIA

The Divine Trap

Novel

Divina Insidia-The Divine Trap

« Amor vincit omnia »

Third Edition :
ISBN-13: 978-1494981228
ISBN-10: 149498122X
Published by CreateSpace Independent Publishing Platform
Copyright © Pascal Roussel
January 2014

Second Edition :
ISBN: 978-3-943687-00-2

DVUB – Deutsche Verlagsunion Berlin GmbH
Neue Mainzer Straße 75
D- 60311 Frankfurt am Main

Published by DVUB – Deutsche Verlagsunion Berlin GmbH
Copyright © DVUB – Deutsche Verlagsunion Berlin GmbH
January 2012

First Edition :
ISBN: 978-2-9535735-8-9
Published by Les Editions Romaines
Copyright © Les Editions Romaines
September 2011

Picture on the cover page taken by Luc Viatour, www.lucnix.be

All rights reserved. No part of this work covered by copyrights may be reproduced or used in any form or by any means, graphic, electronic or mechanical including photocopying, recording, taping or information storage or retrieval systems, without the prior written consent of Pascal Roussel.

Pascal Roussel

DIVINA INSIDIA

The Divine Trap

Novel

ACKNOWLEDGEMENT

The writing of this novel required years of research during which I diligently selected the most reliable sources available. My purpose in writing was twofold , first to provide an entertaining read with a captivating plot, second to provide the reader, what is hopefully an overall insight into a financial world that is both complex and little understood. Much valuable aid was received from many sources in the preparation of this novel none more so than the professional and skillful assistance of Mrs. Françoise Vassort who's experience and exceptional talent is evident as that final important touch to every sentence of the novel. Thank you Françoise, it was a joy working with you, you are an exceptional writer and I hope that you continue to write where you are now.

Finally, due gratitude also to those whose powerful prayers have empowered the realization of this re-edited version and sincere respects to Miss Patricia Kot whose meticulous editing was greatly appreciated.

The following story is a work of fiction. Any resemblance to people, brands, institutions, events or real locations is purely accidental. The characters in this novel are imagined and do not necessarily express the views of the author.

Dedication

To my wife,

without whose support and encouragements this book would not have been possible.

Pascal Roussel

DIVINA INSIDIA

The Divine Trap

Novel

Chapter 1

The old man, cramped in a black cardigan, his huge white beard spreading over the collar, had been sound asleep since the takeoff in Damascus.

When it was time to serve the meal, the flight attendant had tried to wake him up, rather unsuccessfully. Declining the offer with a smile, he had immediately closed his eyes, returning to sleep. Yet he had kept smiling. From time to time, his right hand was gesturing, his shoulders were moving, and it seemed as if he was in delightful agreement with an invisible interlocutor.

Undoubtedly, he was dreaming, and this was quite amusing to the child sitting next to him and quite embarrassing to the child's mother, who was trying to calm him down in vain.

Indeed, he was dreaming. This time, the flight attendant had to insist, gently touching his arm. "Wake up, sir. Could you please bring your seat back all the way forward in preparation for landing?"

"Oh! Yes, yes." He shook himself and complied, and his smile became wider. He patted the cheek of the child, settled in his seat with a sigh of deep satisfaction, and closed his eyes to contemplate once more, for a moment, the intense light that had illuminated his dream.

What a wonderful moment!
At the beginning of the dream, the mixed image of a little boy appeared, opaque and transparent, and looked him, Ahmed, straight in the eyes, intense and tranquil at the same time, before dissolving into this bright light filled with love…
His God was speaking to him! His God was talking to him, to him—Ahmed Mallah!

"You will not allow fear to dominate you! I trust you! What you are going to accomplish will help transform the world. You should know this and prepare yourself, Ahmed Mallah!"

The flight attendant had awakened him at the very moment he was about to take this divine oath, but the main thing had been said. He felt that he was entrusted with a crucial mission and he would live up to it, despite the questions he had.

The aircraft had started its descent toward Seoul, and his presence in this area of the world was no accident. The invitation for the scheduled encounter with two other religious dignitaries had been of some surprise to him, yet he had responded to the invitation without hesitation. The dream he had just confirmed his decision, making him even more impatient.

The aircraft made a smooth landing. Ahmed thanked Allah, put his Koran in his worn-out leather briefcase, which never left his side, and followed the other passengers toward the immigration gate.

The immigration officer, obviously full of self-importance, spoke English fluently. Rather suspiciously, he asked Ahmed to state his identity, his occupation, and the purpose of his visit.

"I am Ahmed Mallah, the grand mufti of Syria."

"Grand mufti—is that your occupation? Would you please be more precise?"

The old man was not fluent in English, yet he answered with a tone that showed he had grasped the double meaning of the question and had been offended.

"A grand mufti, sir, is a high dignitary in the Muslim religion. It is like a cardinal or a chief rabbi." Ahmed spoke in a tone that indicated his answer did not need further explanation.

"What is the purpose of your visit, then?"

"The pleasure of discovering your beautiful country. It is called the land of the morning calm, isn't it?" Ahmed said in a tone that was not without some sarcasm. How could one explain to this officer that he was the highest Muslim authority of Syria? That he was the one who gave guidance to the man of the street as well as to the public figures, the man who checked cultural, judiciary, and political statements to make sure they were conforming to religion. In other words, he was a man whose opinions were respectfully called fatwa.

Because there was some risk in using this term and going into further details, he kept silent, directed a strange limpid expression at the man, and waited. The officer put the official stamps on the passport with a sigh, gave it back to him with an impervious face, and indicated the way forward.

Outside the airport, the damp heat of July was heavy on his shoulders. Fortunately, there was no shortage of taxis. He carried his small cloth suitcase in one hand and his briefcase in the other hand to let the driver know that he could manage by himself, that his luggage was rather light. The cool air in the car made him feel good; he relaxed on his seat, thanking Allah for this safe trip.

*

Eight hours earlier, in Jerusalem, another man was setting off on a journey. After a short and agitated night, His Beatitude Mahran Khoury, the Latin patriarch of Jerusalem and grand prior of the Order of the Holy Sepulchre, had insisted on going to the church before departing. As a man of faith, he wanted to meditate in this holy place.

It was here, in the old city, that the body of Christ had been laid after his death. It was the place of Jesus's crucifixion, and Mahran had dedicated his life to promoting Christian worship in the Middle East.

His order was providing support to schools and many parishes, and he was proud of that. But the conflict in the Holy Land looked insoluble, and he grieved over that. Would he ever see the religions accept one another and support one another? Could a pure faith overcome these cruel and eternal disputes? He wanted to believe it but was still anxious.

Here, in front of Christ's tomb, these questions were harassing him, as well as the pressing request of Friar Giovanni Bassoli. They had first met twenty years ago, back in Rome. The Franciscan friar was living like an ascetic, and his charisma was more than impressive. Whenever they talked, Mahran was more and more convinced that his friend was of a divine essence, and he wanted to believe that Giovanni would later be canonized.

They would occasionally talk to each other, sharing their fervent desire to contemplate the reign of peace in the world. However, ten days ago, their conversation had led them to a decisive turning point. Giovanni, always so meek and respectful, had turned insistent, even commanding.

"Mahran, listen to me! Don't interrupt me and don't argue. You will receive an invitation to go to Korea, and you will accept it. My intuition tells me that it is important."

"Giovanni, I am listening to you and I respect you, but why on earth should I go to Korea? Moreover, I just cannot abandon my duty and all those who count on me! Who will issue this invitation?"

"It will come from an association. I cannot tell you more than this, but the goal is that you will be able to meet a Muslim dignitary and a chief rabbi whose names I have forgotten. You must accept this invitation and meet them! You know very well that I would not bother you so if not for the sake of a major project!"

"All right, all right! When will this invitation come to me?"

"Check your mail and be ready to go. That is all I can tell you."

Mahran took leave of his friend with great perplexity. The next day the invitation arrived. On the envelope, the name of the organization was printed in blue: Religious Peace Organization. The text made the purpose clear—"to organize and facilitate discreet meetings among religious authorities from the Holy Land, where ongoing conflicts continue." These meetings would be protected from any media interference.

The first meeting would be held in Korea, for reasons which were explained in detail. "Since time immemorial, the Koreans have been faithful to God, the creator of all things as the primary ancestor, and just as all numbers start from one, they call God 'the One.' This country, over its five-thousand-year history, has never invaded any other nation, and all religions are also represented there, just as in the Holy Land. This peninsula has had its share of suffering too. The nation is divided into two: the northern population lives under the oppression of a harsh Stalinist regime, whereas in the south the economy has taken off miraculously."

The purpose of the organization was crystal clear: to facilitate interreligious dialogue, the only way to establish a lasting world peace. It had thus invited the grand mufti of Syria and the chief rabbi of Jerusalem, as well as the patriarch of Jerusalem.

The patriarch did not hesitate too long. He did not believe in mere coincidences, and even if he could not figure out how the trip could be useful in the short run, how could he ignore the request of his friend? Moreover, the Lord often works in mysterious ways. He thus called the representative of the Religious Peace Organization and confirmed that he would go. He then learned that he was the first to give a positive answer. His saying yes would help convince the two other dignitaries. He then informed his superiors by mail, indicating the exact address of the meeting, and bought his airplane ticket. He landed in Seoul on Saturday, July 3, 2010, around eight thirty in the morning, a few hours before the grand mufti of Syria.

*

Moshe Aboudaram, the Ashkenazi chief rabbi of Israel, read the invitation of the Religious Peace Organization three times, and he could not refrain from having some doubts. The invitation had arrived the day before, and he had not yet made the decision to accept it. After all, it was an important journey. It would take him two hours to reach the Tel Aviv airport, and a direct flight from Tel Aviv to Seoul was more than unlikely. Therefore, before undertaking the required steps, he thought he'd better call Mahran Khoury, whose name appeared on the list of participants. How did he react to this surprising proposal, and did he intend to give a positive answer?

The name of the organization looked impressive, but did he see it as serious?

Mahran's answer was straightforward. "I am in a hurry, but yes, I shall definitely go to Seoul. It will be a flying visit, since I am needed in Jerusalem on the seventh."

The patriarch apparently had a strong interest in the meeting and saw it as significant, and he did not question the seriousness of the organization. Reassured by these words, Moshe decided to leave as soon as possible and take a few days of vacation for himself.

How long had he continued without taking rest, being overburdened by his tasks? Life in Jerusalem was exhausting, with the unremitting noise of the streets and the daunting anxiety, which was there night and day. Yes, indeed, a forty-eight-hour escape would help him find solace and attend the scheduled meeting with a clear and bright mind. Last but not least, such a meeting was impossible in the Holy Land, where a thousand ears occupied each square inch of space. It would be an illusion to think that such a meeting could be kept secret here.

It was ninety-four degrees in the shade when he left Jerusalem, so the heat in Seoul was not a surprise for him. He went to the headquarters of the Religious Peace Organization, where he was gracefully and heartily welcomed. Immediately, there was a sense of harmony and shared convictions. God had created a world of love; the bloody conflicts that shattered this world absolutely had to be eradicated. There was a general consensus on this point. They agreed to spend the next morning together, and the meeting was scheduled for two o'clock.

*

The chief rabbi arrived first, around one thirty, at the typically small Korean house that had been chosen for the meeting. One member of the organization accompanied him as a facilitator to ensure a problem-free stay. The house was a property of the Religious Peace Organization; located in the Dohwa-dong district, it was cool and calm. In the stone house, one could forget the damp heat of the city.

The front door opened onto a narrow and dark corridor, at the far end of which a second door led to the basement. On the right-hand side of the corridor, a third door gave access to a fourteen-square-yard meeting room. In the middle of the room, there was a round, sturdy table and six high-backed chairs. With its low ceiling, its narrow window looking out on a tiny garden, and its general decoration, the place looked typically Asian. The only presence emanated from the heavy fragrance of the while lilies in a white vase at the center of the table. All around, it was absolutely quiet.

The patriarch arrived a few minutes later, soon followed by the grand mufti. The three religious leaders congratulated one another and started by praying out loud, one after the other, before beginning their discussion.

In this silent street, crushed by the sun at its zenith, a car had parked in the shade of a group of trees, apparently abandoned.

Ten minutes after the spiritual leaders had arrived, an Asian man got out of the car very slowly and closed the door carefully. He then approached the little house. The neighborhood was deserted, allowing him to leave the vehicle and approach the house unseen. The religious leaders, with their eyes closed, absorbed in their meditation, did not hear the noise of the front door, which opened slowly. The Asian man moved down the corridor and came to the door of the conference room. As agile as an animal, he opened the door of the room where the men were in prayer.

In one leap, he was at the center of the room. Holding a dagger in his right hand, he grasped the head of the facilitator and slit his throat. The man fell, knocking over a chair. The three others could hardly understand what was going on. The patriarch uttered a hoarse sound and folded his knees; a red spatter of blood splashed on the walls. The grand mufti made a sign to the rabbi. Did he beg for protection? The latter, his eyes bulging, saw the mufti stumble before he himself fell down. None of them had truly seen the face of the killer.

They had collapsed and were lying on the floor. No other noise could be heard but the disgusting gurgling of the blood flowing from throats and spilling all over the floor, chairs, and table; the quadruple murder had not even taken three minutes, three minutes of mad fury. Shim Jon Gol beheld his work with a smile of satisfaction. To kill four men, three of whom were rather elderly, was a beginner's task, and a beginner he was not. He would not fail to pose a question to those who made this decision: why him? He had been a member of the North Korean Special Security Forces for over ten years and had a brilliant service record. To steal the car had just been a game; to kill these foreigners had been a joke. Right now he only had one regret, that the victims had not even had the time to be afraid. Too bad. The point, however, was to finish the task and vanish without leaving any trace. A few details still had to be taken care of.

First of all, he had to abundantly cover the three holy books—the Christian Bible, the Jewish Bible, and the Koran—with the blood of their owners. Shim Jon Gol made an expressive grimace; he did not like to get his hands dirty. Then, following his instructions, he took a vial out of his pocket, opened it, and poured the liquid over them. Finally, he set fire to everything with a simple lighter.

The combustion was spectacular, and soon only a heap of ashes remained. He took some of it with his knife and filled the vial, which still contained a small amount of the highly flammable liquid. He then closed it and put it back in his pocket, but not without first carefully wrapping it up.

It would not be possible to preserve the peaceful character of the little house; the table started to burn too. This would take too much time. His boss had been very clear: "The product I give you is very powerful and very expensive—nano-thermite. Do you know what that is? It is what the Mossad used to blow up the World Trade Center on September 11, 2001. So please be quick; you have exactly five minutes to save your life."

It was unnecessary to insist on these five minutes. It was more than he needed, and in any case, danger was a real tonic for him. As for this famous terrorist attack in the United States, it may well have been organized, as his boss stated, by the Israeli secret services or by anybody else; he did not really care. The main thing for him was that a few more Americans had been destroyed.

He went to the basement, put the explosive near the gas-fired boiler, set up the tiny detonator, returned to his car in the deserted street, and drove away like a Sunday driver.

He could feel the violence of the explosion a few hundred yards away. He then lit a cigarette and his smile became wider.

*

The same day, the postal services, always steady and reliable, processed a small cardboard box, which could contain chocolates or a highly suspect flask. Nobody would imagine the latter unless gifted with an overactive imagination. The question remained yet and required a precise answer: why had Shim Jon Gol been chosen for a mission that was insignificant as well as nonsensical?
Thousands of miles away, a small flask of glass, bearing occult signs, arrived at its destination. Someone recovered it, someone who was called an "unknown superior."

This person, after having been informed by his faithful contacts in Vatican City about the upcoming encounter of religious leaders, had immediately realized how much this meeting would serve his purpose. These stupid clergies worshipping a losing God! Yes, they would serve the plans of his family! Generations of alliances with the victor had already brought them fortune and power.

The man was already imagining how he would use the content of the flask during the next ceremony. He did not have so much time left to fulfill the great scheme of his invisible ally, and in no way would he let the situation escape his control. The sacrifice of these dignitaries was an offering to the light he worshipped, the light that enabled him to triumph.

Chapter 2

"Oh, Mummy! Such beautiful stamps! They are pure magic! Where did they come from? Will you give them to me?" The twelve-year-old boy was trying to take the envelope from the hands of his mother.

"Nicolas! You and your 'magic'! Go! You will miss the school bus, and I shall not be driving you. We shall talk about these stamps tonight. And don't forget your uncle is coming for dinner; do your homework as soon as you get home."

Anne had found the letter in the morning mail. Posted in Moscow, the letter was bearing stamps representing Red Square's famous basilica of St. Basil the Blessed. The address was correct: Anne Standfort, Centralbahnplatz 7, Basel, Switzerland. Who on earth would write to her from Moscow, where she didn't know anybody?

Despite the work waiting for her, she took the time to sit in an armchair in the living room and opened the envelope. The letter was handwritten on quality paper, and the handwriting was assured, wide, and high. It weighed at least one hundred grams, thought Anne, who correlated the weight and the number of stamps put on the envelope. Dated September 21, 2010, it started with "Dear Anne."

The sender knew her, then? More and more puzzled, she kept reading:

Forgive me for being so familiar and allow me to call you from the beginning by your first name. Yes, Anne, I know you. Or more precisely, I took the liberty of reading your books on numerous occasions, and therefore I know how elegant your style is. I also know your tact, your discretion, and the fineness of the biographies you write. Any person, however famous she may be, could only rejoice to have her story told by you.

I know that you are a respected freelance journalist. I know your age and your family situation. I know the name of your husband as well as his professional situation in the bank. I know that he is the manager of the UBS agency on the Aeschenplatz and that your boy is twelve years old. Please don't be severe with me! If I seem to be indiscrete, it is because of the mission that I would like to propose to you.

I have taken the decision to entrust you with the writing of my biography, and with all false humility put aside, I assure you that I am a very important person whose power has no limits. I am in full possession of my faculties, believe me, and in order to make my proposal more tangible, I shall send you on September 28 a gift that will give you an idea of the level of my expectations. Before that, you'd better have a glance at the building facing you, the Bank of International Settlements. I spent so many hours there.

Let me conclude with a reliable piece of information: by September 28, the put and call options connected to gold on the Comex market will expire and once again my "friends" will have to intervene. We can talk about it later. I am looking forward to seeing you!

A former unknown superior

Anne had to read the letter a couple of times. Her hands were clammy and shaking convulsively. What was she afraid of? What was the meaning of all this? Conflicting feelings prevented her from thinking peacefully.

To think that the author was a lunatic was too simple. He would be a very learned lunatic and particularly well organized. Why did he choose her? Was it because her husband was working in a bank? What about the information on gold? What did she have to do with that?

If he had collected so much information, he should be well informed that finance was absolutely not her cup of tea. It was a field beyond her understanding, ruled by laws that were not natural, rules that were complex and had been created by men and for men.

A strange sensation, which she could not explain, had somehow taken hold of her. It was as if this stranger had entered her life without permission and a sudden danger was around.

She stood up, came close to the window, and looked at the famous "black tower." The severe architecture of the building made her feel even worse. What if Hans, with his position as a banker, had something to do, even unknowingly, with this case? Not long ago, he had proudly announced to her that he would be taking on new responsibilities. It could be that someone may try to influence him through her! Such a tactic made sense. Of course, it would have been good to talk to him about it, but she could already guess his comments: "How can you be so naive, darling? Do you really believe this present? What kind of present, by the way? Will it be a bouquet of roses? The usual present of a gentleman whom you seduced without being aware of it, which would not be a surprise, I should say."

He would take her in his arms, and he would gently tease her. Hans was a strong man, his feet well-grounded in the foundation of his convictions and even if she was more balanced in her judgments, she loved him and refrained from disagreeing with him.

Of course, since Nicolas had seen the letter and the stamps, the event would not remain secret, but for the moment at least, she thought it would be wiser to look indifferent. The more she thought about it, the more she felt that Hans had something to do with this offer. If not, how was it possible to explain why she had been chosen? As a media professional, she knew that true investigative journalists had become very rare, and most of her colleagues limited themselves to copying and pasting agency stories. The competition of the Internet and television, in addition to the decrease of young readers, partly accounted for the crisis that the media world was going through. There had been massive layoffs in the major newspapers as they fought for their survival. Fewer journalists were being hired, and they did not have enough time to make personal investigations. Moreover, no one would dare bypass the editorial line because the prospect of being fired was constantly preying upon their minds. Even so, she was not the only one to do a good job.

She pulled herself together, mobilizing all her wisdom. Her brother would probably be a better adviser, but she would choose another moment to talk to him about that.

On the one hand, Hans was a calm person who read the media as if it were the Bible, and on the other hand, John was skeptical and saw conspiracies everywhere. If the letter that had just arrived became the center of conversation, the evening was likely to be animated, and she was not in the mood to put up with that.

She put the letter back in its envelope and left it on the pedestal table at the entrance, though she carefully covered it up under a heap of flyers. With a peaceful mind, she would have to figure out what looked like a mystery but could also be a threat. Who was behind it? Was it only one person or a group? There was no doubt that this mail had been addressed to her personally, so what kind of trap was this offer hiding? Anne had a sound mind. She was not usually suspicious. In this case, however, an unpleasant feeling was hanging around, and she refused to consider that there was merely a professional and financial dimension to this seemingly interesting proposal.

*

Nicolas was a fan of stamps. In fact, he had been thinking about the magical stamps all day. He had talked about them to his buddies, describing the superb colors in detail. So without hesitation when he got home, he threw his satchel at the feet of the mezzanine, searched in the heap of advertisements, found the envelope, and started to take the stamps away. Naturally, he also took the letter out and read it. He read it a couple of times, just like his mother. What he mostly understood was that she would receive a present. What kind of present, he wondered. His mother liked flowers, but she also liked beautiful furniture, nice dresses, traveling, receptions, and many other things too vague for him. Moreover, the familiar tone also caught his attention, it looked like the "unknown gentleman" knew his mother. That was strange, but it could not in itself disturb a joyful and peaceful boy like Nicolas. Still, the mystery of the letter occupied him intensely.

That is why he trumpeted the news to his father when Hans came home. "Dad!" Mummy will receive a present from a mystery man! I think it's weird that she gets a present from an unknown person, don't you agree, Daddy?"

Nicolas gave the letter to Hans, who read it, frowning, in front of an upset Anne. He asked to see the envelope, which he turned around and around. Finally he concluded, "This joke is in bad taste. He did not even have the courage to sign it. Another lunatic!"

"A lunatic? Do you really mean it?"

"Sure I do! Do your clients usually talk to you with this offhand tone?"

"No, they don't, and I admit that it bothers me."

"And I won't even mention this story of a present to be offered to you! If you work for him, it should not be for a present but for wages. On top of all that, he allows himself to be a modern-day Nostradamus by making prophecies on the price of gold. No, no, believe me, this guy is crazy."

He made a ball of the letter and its envelope and threw it in the trash.

"Anne, please don't talk about it to your brother. He will speak again of a nuclear war and go on for at least two hours!"

"I did not intend to; don't worry about it. On your side, whatever turn our conversation takes, I would like you to remain calm. John is my brother. I have only him, and I have few occasions to see him. I am looking forward to having a pleasant evening."

"All right, darling. I shall do anything to please you. Moreover, your cooking smells so good that we should not damage the pleasure of the palate with a pointless discussion." He expressed his promise by gently kissing her, and Anne smiled. Hans was definitely a loving man, despite his small shortcomings.

Neither of them noticed the darkening expression on Nicolas' face.

*

John arrived a little before seven o'clock, as scheduled. The adults had an aperitif, and Nicolas was offered orange juice. Despite the lack of any profound conversation, the dinner went on in a warm atmosphere. Anne, having a passion for gastronomy, collected recipes from all around the world. She added her personal touch, and Hans trumpeted to anyone ready to hear it that Basel's best restaurant was located at number seven of the Centralbahnplatz! This evening particularly, knowing the delicate palate of John, she had outdone herself. After a salmon mousse on toast, she served her famous "seven o'clock leg of mutton" accompanied with pommes dauphines and fresh salad. Having eaten their fill, they skipped the dessert and were sipping their coffee while talking.

None of the adults had noticed the impatience of the child, who had been giggling on his chair for a while. It was thus a complete surprise when Nicolas declared, "You know, Uncle John, Mummy will receive a present from a man she does not know!"

"Oh! Well? My seductive sister has had another hit?" John was laughing with good heart.

Anne tried to play down the situation. "This is a nonsensical joke of no importance."

But Nicolas, who was proud of having read the letter and wanted at all costs to catch the interest of his uncle, ignored the angry eyes of his father and continued. "It came from Russia. Mummy gave the stamps to me. This man says that he knows her and that she is his friend. Uncle John, I find that strange. He sells gold in the black tower, just in front of our house. Do you believe that he will give gold to Mummy, Uncle John?" Nothing else was needed to make John utterly excited. As a cultivated person, hungry for news, he would explore the Internet, compare sources, and sort out the different new stories. If some people, including Hans, thought of him as a conspiracy nut, he didn't care. No matter what others thought, he was extremely knowledgeable and was proud of it. Verifying information was a citizen's duty, he felt.

There was a moment of embarrassment, which Nicolas did not notice. He was not satisfied. "Tell me, Uncle John, is it true that there is a lot of gold in the black tower?"

"No, I don't believe there is so much in there. You see the black tower, as you call it, is a bank, but a different bank from the bank where your dad is working. It is called the Bank of International Settlements. It's the most important bank in the world, but people don't go there for money deposits. Very few people even know of its existence."

"What is its purpose, then?"

"In order to give you an answer, I should first explain to you how a traditional bank works, like the one where your dad is employed."

"Would you please let me explain by myself?" Hans's intervention was polite but adamant. Without knowing John's interpretation, he already guessed that it would not be appropriate, so he continued to Nicolas, "Everybody must earn money to live, but if we keep that money in our house, there is a risk that thieves might come and steal it. This money is therefore deposited in a bank, which keeps it safe and gives it back to us whenever we need it. Furthermore, the bankers pay interest on the money that they keep for people. The longer the money stays in the bank, the more interest it yields. In this way, people's money is protected and it allows them to have more of it. The bank can also lend money to people who need some, for example, to buy a car or a house. Do you understand?"

At this point, John could not keep from speaking up. Hans's simple presentation was correct but incomplete. Even if it meant giving Nicolas information that would not be useful for a few more years, it would be better to be complete. "Hans, I believe that your son is old enough that we can go a little further into details."

"Yes, Uncle John, I am old enough. Come on!"

What Anne had feared was about to take place, and she was extremely upset with it. These two men could not help but fight over this topic. Hans thought that being a banker made him understand a truth that John did not believe, and a tiny spark was enough to light the fuse. It was enough to make her doubt their intelligence and, above all, their courtesy. She was tempted to explode, to send her son to bed, and to scold her husband and her brother, who suddenly gave her the impression that they were fighting in a kindergarten school yard.

John, imbued with his mission of instructor, had taken Nicolas by the shoulders. "Listen to me, Nicolas. Let us imagine the following situation: You give 100 Swiss francs to a bank, and the banker says that you can get it back whenever you want. Everything is all right then. Now your friend Philippe wants to borrow 90 francs from this same bank. Without telling you, the bank takes 90 francs from your 100 francs and lends them to your friend. The same day both of you meet in front of the bank. Your friend shows you the 90 francs he has just received, and you show him the paper that the banker gave you that guarantees that you gave 100 francs. We now have a total amount of 190 francs. Money has been multiplied. And it doesn't end there. Your friend can deposit these 90 francs in another bank, which will also take 90 percent of this amount to lend it to a third person. Do you follow me?"

"But, Uncle John, your story is just impossible! If I want to get back my 100 francs, the bank would not able to give it back to me. You must be mistaken."

"No, Nicolas, ask your dad. What I just explained is true. The bank has thousands of clients, and to give you back your money, it will just take it from the bank account of another person."

The face of Nicolas expressed a mixture of doubt and incomprehension. Obviously, this mechanism could hardly be grasped by his child's logic.

John continued, "Originally, you see, bankers were goldsmiths, and the table on which a goldsmith worked was called a *banco*. This is where the word *bank* comes from. In the Middle Ages, these craftsmen kept the gold, which they used to make coins or jewels. Gold owners would traditionally ask the goldsmiths to keep it so that the gold would be safe from thieves, like today, you understand?"

Nicolas nodded with a serious face.

"All right. A person deposited his gold with a goldsmith, who was of course paid for protecting it. The goldsmith gave a receipt to the person, a piece of paper that clearly stated how much gold had been deposited. The receipt guaranteed that the gold was indeed the property of that person. Do you still follow me?"

Nicolas nodded once more; he was all ears.

"Let us consider another situation. Imagine an important person who has to travel with money. He would also be afraid of being attacked and robbed, don't you think?"

Nicolas agreed one more time.

"Suppose he has to buy something. What will he do? Either he takes his money with him and risks being robbed, or he leaves his money with a goldsmith for safekeeping but then has no money to spend. To solve this problem, the tradesmen started to accept, as payments for the goods, the receipts given by the goldsmiths. These receipts were the proof that the buyer truly owned the money necessary to buy what he had just purchased. These receipts are the ancestors of the banknotes we use today. They began to be commonly used to pay for goods, and as a result, the goldsmiths accumulated more and more gold."

"But people could come and take their gold, couldn't they?"

"Of course, but they did it only if they really needed it, since they knew that their gold was safe. The goldsmiths noticed that only 10 percent of the people came to pick up their gold."

"And what happened next?"

"Well, some goldsmiths dedicated more time to keeping coins and giving receipts than to making coins. A fantastic idea then sprouted in their minds, and the idea was to lend out their customers' gold without telling them about it."

Nicolas looked stunned. "Wouldn't that be a lie?"

"Yes, my dear boy, but it was a lie by omission. It was easy, you understand. They just needed to keep a little bit, ten percent for instance, in order to meet the demand. They were then transformed into real bankers. Then the time came when a loan was just about writing a document in which the banker promised to give a certain number of gold coins to the person who was holding this document. This promise was then used as a means for payment. In exchange, the borrower had to pay interest. That interest, on the other hand, had to be paid with true gold coins. Do you understand?"

"Well...not really."

"It is simple: the banker was lending paper and was keeping the gold coins. This is how the bankers became very, very rich. Quite rapidly, there were many more promises than real gold in the safes of the bankers. Moreover, there was no risk for them as long as the number of clients coming to withdraw their gold remained limited. This is the mechanism of the creation of virtual gold, Nicolas."

"Well, Uncle John, this is exactly like your example with Philippe. Without knowing it, Philippe borrows 90 francs from my bank, which created them out of nothing?"

"It is true, except that today we are talking about banknotes, not gold."

Anne was listening, stunned. It is one thing not to let money become too important in life, and she was proud of living that way. But not to pay attention to the mechanisms that rule the financial world seemed to her very incoherent, if not irresponsible, at this very moment. How did Hans see the way John presented his work? He was a man whose statements were always so straight and clear!

If for one reason or another, more than 10 percent of the deposited funds had to be withdrawn or if the short-term loans her bank issued every day were not renewed, her bank ran the risk of going bankrupt, pulling in its fall the people of modest means who had trusted it. No doubt Hans had already foreseen this possible outcome, and Anne wanted to believe that he had good reasons to work in this system. Maybe a point of no return had been reached? Maybe without this scheme, there would be a lack of money, preventing the economy from maintaining itself?

"What about the black tower, then?" asked Nicolas.

"The black tower is there in order to make important decisions. That is all."

"But all those floors just to make decisions; it's a little ridiculous, isn't it?" Depending on his mood, Nicolas had a special gift for remaining stubbornly attached to his first idea.

"Wait! I shall explain everything to you. Now that you have understood how the banks multiply money, I shall explain to you how money was created originally. A bank that has the authority to create money and inject it into the financial system is called a central bank, and the black tower is involved in all that takes place in the banks. So you see, if the government does not have enough money, it must borrow, just like a family, just like anybody. Therefore, it asks the central bank, directly or indirectly, which creates the money needed and lends it to the government."

"But then why can't everybody do the same thing? You just need to print paper and pretend that it's money."

"It is not that simple, even if looks like a game."

"It is difficult to understand, Uncle John, but I think somehow I will manage to get it, even if I have a strange feeling about all of it."

"Yes, Nicolas, it is difficult to understand."

The two men looked at each other with perplexity. This time they felt united in the parental duty. How on earth could they clarify for this child what even for them, despite their knowledge, remained a bit mysterious?

Anne, who was puzzled by the turn of the conversation, insisted, "If I understand well, a 10 franc banknote exists only because someone, somewhere, one day, borrowed 10 francs? If tomorrow all the debts were reimbursed and no one borrowed even a cent, would all the money in circulation disappear?"

"Yes, it is exactly what would happen. Tomorrow, at the till of the supermarket, remember that you pay with the debt of someone. There is no money without debt!"

"And I believed that the safes of the central banks were filled with gold and that there was enough to exchange it against banknotes!"

Hans responded, "My darling, in August 1971 the American president Nixon disconnected currency from gold. In financial terms, it is said that he signed the death warrant of the international monetary system of Bretton Woods."

"So, if I understand well, in the beginning, exchanges were made using gold. Then the goldsmiths created the equivalent of this gold in paper. Then they issued more paper than gold, and finally they suppressed gold? It really looks like the financial world is playing the sorcerer's apprentice for its own enjoyment."

Hans tenderly took his wife by the shoulders, and he was about to continue when John spoke. "Why do you think the central banks don't like gold? Because, unlike electronic money, they cannot create it. Originally, money did not exist and men were bartering. Let me give you a very basic example. Thus, a peasant who desired to get a cup made by the potter gave him two salads in exchange. However, the peasant did not have salads in winter, so there was no possibility for bartering. With the passing of time, universal means of exchange have appeared, and gold coins and money started to spread. The peasant could sell his two salads for a coin, and the potter could sell cup for a coin. The equivalence of the value of the cup against that of two salads was preserved. Nowadays, we pay with banknotes, but the banknote remains a simple means of exchange. However, when a central bank creates too much money and when the commercial banks then multiply it, they dilute the exchange value of the currency. Money is less rare and thus loses its value. As it has less value, more of it is needed to exchange and the prices soar. The cost of two salads is no longer one coin, as it was before the injection of money, but two. And a cup does not cost one coin anymore, but two. Gold is an excellent index of monetary creation because it is universally recognized and is very rare. All the gold extracted from the earth represents a small cube of about twenty-two yards. It does not even cover your grandmother's garden! And the size of this cube increases only about five inches every year."

John could not conclude, obviously carried away by his topic. "When monetary creation increases, spurred by credit, the price of gold must increase because the bankers are not alchemists and cannot create this metal. On the one hand, the banknotes are more and more abundant; on the other hand, this metal remains rare. More banknotes are thus necessary to buy gold. Gold, therefore, plays the role of the canary in the mine that warns miners about the possibility of a firedamp explosion. In order to deter people from being worried, the central banks use diverse techniques to manipulate the price of gold to fall, particularly on the Comex market or on the gold stock exchange of London. It is a little complex, but to make things simple, you should know that these techniques all use the same old principle: in order for the price of gold not to soar excessively, you should just not sell much of it. Since gold is rare, the central banks and their accomplices, such as some commercial banks, have only one means to sell gold massively—sell much more gold than they actually possess. As most of the buyers are trusting and do not intend to keep the gold for very long, they allow the selling bank to maintain the caretaking of the gold that they come to buy. They don't ask to see it and keep it in a safe in their name; thus they do not realize that the gold they just bought does not exist. If all the clients came to ask for their gold and carry it away, they would discover the trick and some major banks would go bankrupt. This will take place one day; people are becoming more and more cautious."

Hans harshly replied, "Things are simpler than that. Gold is a barbarous relic, as the great economist Keynes once said. It does not yield anything and has dropped significantly in value. It is a medieval system, and it is stupid to believe that central banks are still interested in it!"

"It is the gold standard system that Keynes called a barbarous relic, not the metal itself. Having said this, I don't intend to be contentious."

"In any case, the gentleman who wrote the letter said that his friends would intervene on the Comex for gold, but I did not understand it," said Nicolas. Despite the complex turn of John's speech, he had remained very attentive.

His intervention triggered a prompt reaction from John: "I would like to see this letter."

Hans, who felt uneasy with John's speech, replied, "It is impossible. I threw it in the trash can."

Nicolas imperceptibly blushed and, staring at his uncle, said, "I still did not understand very clearly what was being done in the black tower!"

"All the banks of the world are connected to their respective central banks, and all the central banks of the world are in turn connected to a unique bank, the one you call the black tower, on the other side of your street. But as I told you, its exact name is the Bank of International Settlements, or the BIS. It was founded in 1930, is the oldest international financial institution in the world, and offers bank settlements. As it has a central role in finance, its power is huge, but very few people are aware of it."

Hans harshly cut him off. "Unlike you, I work in a bank and I can tell you that the BIS is a respectable Swiss institution that releases reports with recommendations; it does not play any central role. Only people like you, who are fond of conspiracy theories, imagine such nonsensical schemes."

John was gifted with a very powerful memory and, cut to the quick by Hans's words, did not resist the pleasure to show it. "The great American historian Carroll Quigley, mentor of Bill Clinton, was a professor of history at the University of Georgetown and a member of the Council on Foreign Relations. His work *Tragedy and Hope* described in detail the goals of the financial lobby that led to the Bretton Woods agreements. He says, for instance, 'The powers of financial capitalism had another far-reaching aim, nothing less than to create a world system of financial control in private hands able to dominate the political system of each country and the economy of the world as a whole. This system was to be controlled in a feudalist fashion by the central banks of the world acting in concert, by secret agreements arrived at in frequent private meetings and conferences. The apex of the system was to be the Bank for International Settlements in Basel, Switzerland, a private bank owned and controlled by the world's central banks which were themselves private corporations. Each central bank ... sought to dominate its government by its ability to control Treasury loans, to manipulate foreign exchanges, to influence the levels of economic activity in the country, and to influence cooperative politicians by subsequent economic rewards in the business world.'"

Without pause, he continued, "And you're not going to tell me that Professor Quigley is a conspirator? This bank enjoys the same legal status as an embassy. The Swiss police cannot get in there, and the managers have diplomatic immunity. How can you believe that it's merely an ordinary bank?"

Before the situation could deteriorate any further, Anne jumped in. "John, I am sure that Nicolas would be happy for you to tuck him in. It is high time that he go to bed!"

The child did not resist, quickly kissed his parents, and went to his bedroom, dragging his uncle by the hand. When he was in his bedroom, he took the letter out of the drawer of his desk and, without a word, gave it to John.

John sat down on the bed beside Nicolas, trying to master an emotion whose origin was familiar to him and which he did not like. The word *danger* was creeping in his mind and was confirmed by the time he had finished reading the letter. It was not a hoax. The "unknown superiors" were not unknown to him, and his anxiety kept growing, though it was out of the question to instill it in his nephew. "Thanks for showing it to me, Nicolas. It is no doubt a joke, but who knows? Jokes of bad taste exist. Write my mobile phone number in a corner of your school diary. I shall still be in Europe for a month. Call me if you notice anything strange."

"Do you mean dangerous? Dangerous for Mummy?"

"No, don't exaggerate, but nevertheless, we can never be too cautious, can we? Moreover, you are big and you are smart, so I know that I can count on you to watch out, OK?"

"OK, Uncle John. Dad works hard, and when he is here he can have his head in the clouds!"

John was about to leave the room when he noticed a reproduction, an image depicting in black and white a striking Lucifer, albeit with an air of sadness, standing straight and tall, big wings spread out. He seemed to implore the heavens. All of Gustave Doré's mastery of his art seemed concentrated in this picture. John knew his nephew to be gifted with a keen intuition and sensitivity for certain atmospheres, but a picture like this in a little boy's room seemed distinctly out of sync!

"Tell me, Nicolas, who gave you this picture?"

"You like it Uncle John? It's really beautiful isn't it?"

"Well, yes, but tell me who gave it to you."

"I saw it in a shop window and asked mummy if I could have it for my birthday."

"And she agreed?" John asked with obvious surprise.

"Well, I had to work hard to convince her!"

"So tell me, Nicolas, what do you like about the picture?"

"Don't you see? It's Lucifer."

"Yes, I recognized him. But I still do not grasp your fascination."

"But, Uncle, Lucifer is the devil!"

"Right!"

"This artist made him look nice. Normally the devil is imagined to be horrible, but in this picture he...well, he looks like us. It's like the artist has seen him!"

"Well, if you insist. But you should know that often the ugly side of a person is hidden."

"Yes, I know! But you see, Uncle John, when one draws, one can show things one can't see with the eyes."

"Well, OK, perhaps..."

"I find it very interesting to show what one cannot see!"

"And that, my dear boy, I find most disturbing!"

"Oh, Uncle John, don't worry. It's just a picture."

"OK, OK. You are right, my dear Nicolas." He tenderly hugged his nephew, who was exhausted. Nicolas had already undressed and was under the sheets without bothering to put on his pajamas.

John, whilst returning to join his sister, pondered perplexedly on the strange attitude of the little boy.

In the kitchen, Anne was alone and was tidying. John took her in his arms and hugged her. "Promise to keep me informed if this joker reappears."

"Yes, but don't worry too much; it is a hoax of no importance."

"I am not so sure about this, Anne. Behind their benign appearance, those people can behave as fearful predators when their interests are at stake."

Through the window, Anne saw him get into his car and thought that she completely trusted the judgment of her brother. This time was different, however, and the trust placed in him did not bring any comfort to her. A vague anxiety was floating around her, and she knew that she would not be able to share it.

Chapter 3

The next morning, Tuesday, September 28, 2010, Anne was finishing her breakfast when her phone rang. Hans was working and Nicolas was at school. An unknown number appeared on the telephone, and she picked it up.

"May I speak to Mrs. Anne Standfort, please?"

"Anne Standfort speaking."

"Good morning, Mrs. Standfort. I am the general director of the bank Goldstein & Sons. I would like to meet you, Madam. When would that be possible for you?"

The tone was peremptory, and Anne was immediately displeased. "May I ask for what purpose?"

"It is a sensitive question, and I would like to talk to you face to face."

"I see, but I have a very busy schedule. And as I don't have an account in your bank, I therefore fail to see any purpose of our meeting."

"You are mistaken, Madam. You are one of our customers."

"I beg your pardon?"

"A close friend has asked me to open a numbered account in your name, which I personally did. Usually, for this type of account, the identity of the holder is known only to a few employees of the bank. In the present case, I am the only one to know your identity, but this does not mean that you should not legalize the necessary documents."

"Sir, the opening of an account without my permission and without my even being informed about it seems to be more than suspect. Or, and this is more likely, it is a mistake. Somebody must have the same name, I guess?"

"I should say that it is a very unusual kind of transaction, but I am the director of this bank and personally verified that the proceedings are valid, especially since we are dealing with a sum of four hundred million francs."

There was silence. Anne swallowed. The man continued, "I did say four hundred million francs, and I tell you that there is no mistake and the name is really yours. At what time will you be here?"

"I shall be there in thirty minutes."

"That's perfect!" The voice had a sarcastic tone, if Anne was not mistaken, as if the man had said something like, "You have become reasonable at last!"

After the call ended, Anne stood up like a robot and went to look at herself in the mirror in the entrance. She saw herself, pale and disheveled. During the few minutes of this bewildering conversation she had not stopped passing her hand through her hair. Despite her denial, the anxiety had not left her since she had received the letter. And now there was the pressure of this unknown banker plus this unbelievable amount of money. Who was behind all this? Who could believe her to be so corruptible that pressing instructions like this could be given to her?

She drank a big glass of water and, suddenly feeling impatient to elucidate this mystery, prepared herself to go. Hans had to be informed, however. With his usual composure, he would find a rational explanation. But with the anxiety that kept creeping in on her, she already had a foreboding that there was nothing rational in this adventure and, above all, the amount of money which had landed in her bank account. She understood at this moment that this latter detail had to remain nebulous, at least for the moment. As expected, her husband confirmed that the bank was a serious one and specialized in the management of the largest fortunes. He was also personally convinced that this was a mistake that was about to be corrected. Maybe it had already been identified. He offered to go with her, which she refused.

Less than thirty minutes later she entered the bank's offices. An employee invited her to wait for a few moments. She sat in an armchair surrounded by green plants, and she was admiring their luxuriance when her eye was drawn to the huge television screen on the wall facing her. Nonstop news reports were being broadcast from a financial news channel. Anne started, flushed, and unbuttoned her coat. A journalist was explaining that the price of gold had just dropped 2 percent and no plausible explanation had been found.

At that moment, David Goldstein appeared. He greeted Anne very politely and invited her to follow him to his office. She sat in front of him and tried to master her feeling of uneasiness. As if he wanted to give a more theatrical character to the meeting, David Goldstein looked at her for a few moments before he started to speak with a paternalistic tone, his elbows on the desk and his forefingers touching each other.

He took a deep breath and began. "Dear Mrs. Standfort, as I told you, this situation is very unusual indeed. You may be aware that—and this is very different from what you see in movies—a numbered account is not anonymous but is known only to a few persons because an absolute confidentiality has to be guaranteed. In the case which we are discussing, as I said earlier, I am the only one who knows your identity. I understand your feeling, however, when a number is followed by many zeros, and all of this happens to be on a bank account in your name. You do have a few questions, don't you?"

He had a very unpleasant throat laugh and continued on a tone that did not call for reply. "The documents are ready; you have only to sign."

"Sir, with all due respect, I maintain that it must be a mistake. No one owes me such a large amount of money."

"*Owe* may not be the right choice of words, indeed. However this account is completely real and I guarantee that it is absolutely confidential. I just need your signature and a copy of your ID card."

Anne was sweating. He added, "Mrs. Standfort, the person who wired this money belongs to a family that has been a client of my bank for generations. This person is honoring me with the favor of his friendship, and I am not allowed to give his name. However, he informed me that he had explained everything to you by mail."

Again that letter! Since the beginning, Anne had felt that there was a troubling connection between the letter, the announced present, and this money which was being offered. But offered for what reason and in exchange for what, precisely? The mere writer of a book is never paid that much!

"I did receive a letter. It was not signed, and I thought it was a hoax."

"My dear Madam, you will soon learn that when these people talk about money, they are never joking. I shall thus inform him that everything is all right, and I have no doubt that he will very soon contact you."

He presented the documents to Anne, with a pen, and she signed. He gave her some information regarding the management of the account, which she did not remember, and then he stood up. With an icy smile on his face, he motioned toward the doorway with his hand. The meeting was over; it had lasted less than ten minutes.

What Anne was not aware of, for obvious reasons, was that the banker felt an intense satisfaction. Beneath his attitude of a Roman emperor, David Goldstein was a man devoured by ambition. For such a long time, with a never-ending patience, he had been waiting for the opportunity to come closer to the "crowned heads," and he had the feeling that through this affair, which had been entrusted to him in the highest secrecy, he had just made giant steps upward in this hierarchy that he craved to belong to one day.

Anne found herself in the street, feeling completely disoriented. Without thinking, she looked at her watch; it was nine thirty. Again her mobile phone rang.

"Good morning, Anne. Well, did you like my present?" The voice was firm but hoarse, the voice of a long-time smoker.

"Who are you?"

"I am going to answer your questions, Anne, but when you are together with me, around three o'clock. If you leave immediately, you will be able to catch the 12:45 p.m. flight from Geneva to Venice. A return ticket is waiting for you at the airport, and someone will be there to pick you up when you arrive."

"Am I to be ordered about by you?"

"Take the letter with you, the letter that I sent you. It would be hazardous to leave any trace of it."

He had completely ignored her reaction, and she lost her temper. "You do not understand! I do not intend to obey you!"

"It is you who do not understand. It is too late to go back on this. It won't be long before the others discover what I have just done, so we need to act quickly. I have many things to explain to you. Don't forget to take the letter!"

Anne calmed down. By giving her assent to this money, she had trapped herself. She understood in a moment that she had to see things through to the end. "I don't have that letter anymore; I threw it away."

"Are you sure that you destroyed it?"

"I am absolutely sure."

"See you soon!" With that, the unknown caller abruptly hung up.

Anne breathed deeply and decided to tame this anxiety coming from who knew where. After making her decision, she called Hans.

"You're not going to obey him, are you?"

"I don't really have a choice. I want to understand what this is all about."

"When are you coming back?"

"I shall be back this evening. I have a return ticket. Will you be able to pick up Nicolas at school?"

"Yes, be careful."

"Of course! I love you."

"I love you too, darling."

Anne knew that, from this moment until she came back, Hans would be scared. But he trusted her and had never undermined any of her projects or opposed her decisions. They were a true couple. They knew it, and they appreciated the value of it.

On the way, she called John. He did not confess to having read the letter, but he insisted on seeing her the next day, and she promised to do so.

No doubt the mysterious man had chosen the furthest airport from Basel in order to increase the pressure on her and thus test her resolve but by 12:45, she was in the airplane, after having found a return ticket to Geneva in her name. Firmly determined to remain calm, she started a session of deep breathing, as she usually did in difficult circumstances.

When she arrived in Venice, she was clear minded and focused. An Asian man was waiting with her name on a sign. He asked her in English to follow him and led her to a pier where a luxury boat was waiting for them. The trip lasted about thirty minutes; they did not exchange a word.

Anne remembered her first visit to Venice, during a weekend with Hans, before the birth of Nicolas. She was very sensitive to the spiritual atmosphere of a place, and she had felt no attraction to this city. Today, again, she felt that a bad spirit was haunting the City of the Doges. As with the first time, the charm of the legendary city had no effect on her.

The boat stopped in front of a splendid palace. This was the residence, then, of the "unknown superior" she was about to meet? She followed her guide, going through several gorgeous corridors, until they reached a large rotunda. The ceiling was very high and was painted in the Italian style. Masterpieces decorated the walls, the floor was in marble of different colors, and there was a dim light everywhere.

In the middle of the room, a huge table was covered with brocade. Three books could be seen in a corner of the table. Despite the beauty of the place, Anne shivered. Was she feeling cold or was she paralyzed by the solemn atmosphere? Before she could answer this question, an old man had already approached her, walking with the help of a cane. She had time to observe the elegance of the dark suit, the deep wrinkles of the face, and above all the eyes, swollen by what was either a purulent conjunctivitis or a no less aggressive psoriasis.

"Good afternoon, Anne, I hope that you had a nice journey." It was the same voice, hoarse and imperative. He had a pleasant smile.

"Yes, thank you. But please, let us get to the point. Why am I here and who are you?"

"You are nervous. I can understand this."

"I am not nervous. I understand that I am involved in something and that I have to see it through to the end. The point, therefore, is not about my nerves, which I control very well, but about my time, which I don't feel like wasting in exhausting performances."

"All right!" He was smiling again and seemed to be delighted by Anne's severe judgment. "We shall go straight to the point. I shall answer your questions, but in the right order. As I told you in my letter, I expect you to help me with your book-writing talent."

"The story of your life?"

"No, not exactly... But before anything, Anne, are you hungry?"

"No, thank you."

"We have quite some time ahead of us."

"I know, but tea will be enough."

"As you like." The old man dialed an internal phone number, and immediately a butler appeared. He gave him his instructions, and hardly three minutes later, as if everything was already prepared in an adjacent room, he came back with a tray gorgeously filled with tea, biscuits, and chocolates. He served everything and left the room.

"Tell me, what did you think about my present?"

"I don't understand why you convinced your friend Mr. Goldstein to open an account in my name in his bank and why you credited it with such a large amount."

"Know that Mr. Goldstein is not my friend!" He could not control a movement of displeasure that Anne was unable to explain. "In my world, there is no such thing as friendship. David Goldstein knows perfectly well how much power I hold; besides that, he is so adamant in his objective, which is to come closer to the oligarchic families. He also has the dream of marrying one of my nieces, which would bring him within the limited circle of the decision makers. For over a century his family has been toying with the project of uniting with mine, but this will never happen. Having said this, I am delighted to learn that the amount put on your account seems to be important to you."

"Our opinions about that may not match."

"This amount, Anne, is not as important as you imagine. Are you interested in numerology?"

Now what? Had she traveled all the way to Venice just to hear about numerology? Why not astrology? She replied quite harshly, "I am not really interested."

"Too bad! I have chosen an amount that starts with the number four. You probably did not pay attention to it, did you? In the monotheist religions, which are based on the Bible or on the Koran, this number always symbolizes a conditional effort to separate from evil and return to good." This last sentence had been pronounced like a universal truth known to all.

"You are really amazing. I still don't know your name, and I know nothing of your motivations. You are obviously a rich and powerful man, beyond what one may imagine, and thus deeply materialist. And you talk to me about spirituality and returning to good. Should I conclude that you are you living with evil?" Anne, who was trying to take the lead in the discussion by being provocative, understood that it would be useless.

The old man, immersed in his thoughts, was unreachable. "It is true that those who reach the first level of wealth are quite often obsessed by material possessions. The thought of purchasing extraordinary goods stimulates them and strengthens their feeling of superiority. These people are often in magazines like *Forbes*. They like to be talked about; this flatters their primary ego. But their fortune is ephemeral. If there is a crisis, they collapse and disappear. As you know only this kind of billionaire, you think that people like me are materialists. Don't be mistaken! When one reaches a level of wealth such as mine, the mere acquisition of any material possession, however important it may be, no longer brings satisfaction, and when one rules over the visible world, one desires to reach the superior level—to control the invisible world! And believe me, it is perfectly possible for someone like me to come to terms with the invisible forces. They need very powerful people to maintain their own survival."

There was a silence, which she refrained from breaking.

"I don't want to go any further into this domain during our first meeting. We have time."

Anne was more and more curious. Here were the elements, without a doubt, with which she could produce an article, or even a book, of quality. She already imagined very well how to report this misadventure, which had everything to captivate a large audience. But there remained some shadow, and it was not a small thing. Of course, it was easy to believe that this man had lost his reason because of his age, or because of memories of some lost causes, or perhaps because he wanted revenge, who could say? But deep inside herself, she was convinced that there remained key elements to be explained, and this made her feel even more strongly the necessity of being attentive and, above all, clear sighted.

"You claim that the billionaires whose names are mentioned in *Forbes* don't represent anything compared to certain families, including yours. Why do the names of these families appear nowhere, and how can you be so rich? Are you speculating on the stock exchange?"

He laughed loudly, but immediately a loose cough shook him for a long moment. After he regained himself, he responded. "The stock exchange, you say? It is dominated by computer programs that buy and sell among themselves at the speed of light. The stock exchange is no longer a good place for investors to make money. All that is mere illusion! Your candor makes you so lovable, my dear Anne; it was one of my reasons for choosing you, by the way. You belong to the camp of those who are dominated. You think like them. You speak their language, and you will do a better job than I would of making things clear."

Anne could have been offended by the condescending tone, but she was more and more interested, and thus she refrained from showing offence. "All right, enlighten me then!"

"Enlighten you? The choice of words is interesting. You should know that the invisible forces I just mentioned claim to be light bearers and that those who followed them called themselves illuminated. Forgive me for this small digression. Let me come back to the names of the oligarchic families. These names are not unknown, Anne. Their level of power and their real wealth are simply underestimated. We control, directly or indirectly, the magazines like the one you just mentioned. Our fortunes, which took several centuries to build up, have branched out so much that it is now impossible to evaluate, and we deter anyone from trying to discover it. Absolute discretion is one of the keys of our power, but to start, I shall explain to you how my family became so rich."

The old man stood up with difficulty and leaning on his cane, he went to the table. "Come here! Open these books. I have placed a bookmark in each of them, and on the corresponding page, the interesting excerpt is highlighted. Read them out loud, please."

Anne came closer to him and took the first book of the pile. To her great surprise, it was the Old Testament. She opened at the indicated page and read Ezekiel 18:12–13. "If he oppresses the poor and needy, commits robbery, does not restore the pledge, lifts up his eyes to idols, commits abomination, lends at interest, and takes profit; shall he then live? He shall not live. He has done all these abominations; he shall surely die; his blood shall be upon himself!"

The young woman detached her eyes from the holy book and turned them toward the old man but could not face his eyes.

Seeing her incomprehension, he declared slowly and mysteriously. "You don't understand that this is precisely the key of the power of the oligarchic families? Don't you find it amazing that the interest-bearing loan, or usury as it was called in the past, is considered a crime so serious that it deserves the death penalty? Do you not think it a strange thing that God is interested in finance, which we don't expect to be among the spiritual concerns of the Bible?"

Anne was perplexed. Hans, the man she so tenderly loved, the father of Nicolas, was working in a bank. His daily activities dealt with interest-bearing loans! Of course, the point here was about exaggerated interest, which was not the case of the bank where Hans was employed. She wanted to believe it with all her heart.

She took the second book; it was the Koran. She went through it to the indicated page. It was the first time she had ever opened the holy book, and she read Surah Two, Al-Baqarah 275–80. "Those who consume interest cannot stand [on the Day of Resurrection] except as one stands who is being beaten by Satan into insanity. That is because they say, 'Trade is [just] like interest.' But Allah has permitted trade and has forbidden interest. So whoever has received an admonition from his Lord and desists may have what is past, and his affair rests with Allah. But whoever returns to [dealing in interest or usury] those are the companions of the Fire; they will abide eternally therein."

"You see, Anne, it is the same thing. God prohibits the interest-bearing loan; Islamic finance is actually grounded in this principle!" There was a tone of victory in this statement.

Anne took the last book. This time it was the New Testament, and she read John 2:13–16. "And the Jews' Passover was at hand, and Jesus went up to Jerusalem. And found in the temple those that sold oxen and sheep and doves, and the changers of money sitting: And when he had made a scourge of small cords, he drove them all out of the temple, and the sheep, and the oxen; and poured out the changers' money, and overthrew the tables; and said unto them that sold doves, Take these things hence; make not my Father's house a house of merchandise."

"Did you know, Anne, that there is no other moment in his public life where Jesus expressed such anger? The money changers were the bankers of that time."

Anne did not know what to say. She could imagine thousands of crimes, a criminal activity making millions, anything except a transaction as normal as an interest-bearing loan. The present received in the morning showed the power of the old man facing her. Was he a lunatic? Or was he on the verge of becoming crazy?

As if he were reading her mind, he continued: "It is perfectly normal that an interest-bearing loan seems not only habitual but normal. For several centuries, we have taken care that no one may ever challenge this. Your husband lends money every day. When he lends a hundred, he is not conscience-stricken to ask the borrower to reimburse one hundred and twenty. This is seen as a token for the service that was provided and also to compensate the risk taken of not being able to be reimbursed."

"That could be, but I still fail to see what your point is, unless there exists a mysterious formula that leads, always through interest, to the building of fortunes like yours."

"Here is the great secret: the interest-bearing loan automatically and, above all, irremediably concentrates money in the hands of the most important lenders. At its root, it is a simple mathematical calculation, but it is first of all a malodorous and unavoidable mechanism. To start with, one has to observe the exponential law that applies to interest. Though the human brain easily conceives linear progressions—when something is doubled or tripled—exponential growth is something much more difficult to grasp."

He suddenly started to burst out laughing, but this ended with a cough. His voice became even hoarser. "This had a very high cost for King Shiram. Do you know the legend of Sissa?"

Anne shook her head.

"Sissa was the man who invented the game of chess; one day he asked King Shiram to offer him a symbolic reward for having given him the strategic and military satisfaction of this hobby. Sissa wanted to be offered grains of rice, spread on the sixty-four squares of the game—one grain of rice on the first square, two grains on the second, four grains on the third, eight grains on the fourth, sixteen on the fifth, and so on and so forth, each time doubling the number of grains. The king accepted and laughed about the modesty of the inventor. Unfortunately, by following this exponential law, the monarch came to understand with horror that he would have to give him 18 billion billion grains—more than one thousand years' worth of the world's production! You see, Anne, it is the same with interest. If the amount first grows slowly, with time it becomes astronomical. Suppose someone borrows 1,000 francs at a compound rate of 4 percent each year. By making his payment once a year for eighteen years, he will have to pay the double of the borrowed amount, or 2,000 francs. If the payment is made over fifty-eight years, he will pay 10,000 francs, ten times the borrowed amount. In 116 years, the amount will be 100,000 francs; in 200 years, it will be 255,000 francs."

Anne was astounded, and he continued without taking a breath, as if he were controlled by an unstoppable mechanism. "In 300 years, he will pay 129,000 times the initial amount, and so on! Of course, no one borrows over a period of hundreds of years, but my family has kept lending more and more money, for several centuries. When these loans cover such a long span of time, the capital is multiplied by a factor that no one can imagine. My family started lending gold about eight hundred years ago, keeping the owners in ignorance. Then money was lent to monarchs in order to finance their wars, and both sides received money—which of course they did not know. With the collaboration of the other oligarchic families, my family saw to it that this gold was no longer used in exchanges but was replaced by debt money. All over the world, countries must borrow from private banks in order to finance themselves. Finally, there exists an absolute rule that protects our fortune and keeps it from being dispersed, and this concerns our marriages. In our circles, no one chooses his or her spouse. This is completely decided based on the interests of the family—or clan, should I say? — and the heirs are practically designated in the cradle."

"And what if all that was changed? What is preventing a country from issuing a currency that is not backed by debts?" Anne was again standing up to her interlocutor and was challenging him with a somewhat mischievous tone.

"In principle, there is no obstacle. But they don't do it—we make sure of that! In 1881, the American president Garfield was assassinated after vehemently opposing the major bankers. In 1865, Lincoln was also assassinated after he dared issue his own currency without using our services. And, more recently, we were challenged by President Kennedy. On June 4, 1963, Executive Order 11110 was signed by President Kennedy, directing the US Treasury to issue a new US currency. This new currency was to be backed by silver coins held in the safes of the US Treasury. This government thus issued banknotes without borrowing and without any relationship to debt. With Kennedy's executive order, $4.3 billion was thus circulated as two- and five-dollar bills. As you know, five months later, he was assassinated. He had attempted to break out of the mold. His challenging the power of the families, through several decisions he made, upset the families. They thus asked the CIA to deal with the situation. The day after he died, this executive order was cancelled and the banknotes were withdrawn."

"But what if the borrowers don't pay?" Anne was trying to find a weak point.

"Most loans are made against a security that can easily be seized. Moreover, the gains realized on the majority of loans largely compensate the possible losses. Anne, do you know that half of the world's population owns only 1 percent of its wealth! And only 10 percent of the wealthiest people own 80 percent of the wealth of households! Is it a mere coincidence if wealth is concentrated so strongly in such a small number of hands?"

Anne was growing impatient. What was the bottom line? He liked to display his power, but apparently not for his personal glory. So it was probably about the book that she would have to write. But apart from this work and the release of the book, the final objective was not yet clear to her. He had been connected to this world and was still a part of it. Was he really willing to denounce it? Was he trying to eradicate it, perhaps? And what was her role in this project? Why had she been chosen? She moved in her armchair and politely repressed her desire to look at her watch.

He did not seem to notice her attitude and continued.

"Now that I have explained to you that, over the years, the exponential growth works inexorably and the perceived interest becomes considerable, I would like you to understand why this same interest converges toward the major lenders, and I shall try to express this mathematical calculation through images."

Settling back in this chair, he began. "A long time ago, there was a village in which ten families were living. They knew nothing about money and were living through bartering only. This was not very convenient, however. For instance, in winter, a farmer had no crops to exchange. But there was a spirit of solidarity, and when a family needed support, it could rely on the others. Life went on peacefully until the day when a stranger arrived in the village. The man was dressed in black; he gathered all the families and told them that he had a wonderful invention that would greatly facilitate their exchanges. This invention had already been useful elsewhere, greatly improving the well-being of all. He showed the people a bag containing gold coins, and he gave out one hundred coins to each family. Barter would be infinitely easier, he told them, if instead of exchanging the products, they used one or several coins. In this way, one could exchange a jug of milk for two coins or exchange a coin for bread. The people were fascinated and were ready to believe the stranger and follow his advice. The system spread quickly, and from then on, a price was given to each object. Once the system was put into place, the stranger gathered the families and told them that the precious service he had offered them deserved some reward. In one year, it would be good if each of the families, having received one hundred coins as a loan, could give back the hundred coins plus ten coins in gratitude. A few protests mounted—how could they give back ten coins when they had received only one hundred? 'Don't worry,' the man told them, 'I trust you, and I am sure that you will find the means to repay me. For those who cannot manage, I shall find another solution.'"

Anne was listening intently, and the man continued his story. "After he was gone, life in the village changed overnight. Cooperation gave way to competition. Obsessed with repaying the loan, people became less and less generous. In fact, in order to be able to repay the capital and the interest, what other means did they have than taking coins from others? One year later, as had been announced, the stranger came back, and nine families could proudly repay the capital and the interest, but the last family had only ten coins left. He then demanded to seize their house as compensation. In just a year, the implacable mechanism of interest had done its work and the wealth of the whole village was held by an ever smaller number of hands. You see, Anne, it is a simple story, but on the world scale, it is exactly what happens."

Anne let him expound all theory, expecting to take control of the conversation as soon as possible. At the first opportunity Anne comments;

"But gold coins have not been used for a long time. Today payments are made with money backed by debt and the central banks create this money in sufficient amounts in order to avoid this competition."

Anne had not forgotten the explanations given by her brother. The old man was talking to her as if she was a child who is told stories illustrating the facts in a simple and clear manner. She felt vaguely ridiculous, not to mention that time was passing and that she still failed to see the real purpose of this conversation hundreds of miles from home.

Without being bothered by Anne's impatient tone, he kept talking: "It is true, but money is created from debt. Thus, quite logically, it is impossible to issue money so that everybody can have enough of it. A banknote of ten francs is created based on a debt of ten francs, and this debt must be reimbursed with interest. It is a never-ending spiral. In complete ignorance, people are fighting among themselves every day to take from one another the money necessary to repay the major lenders. You see the analogy with my story! The village is humanity. The stranger symbolizes the oligarchic families capable of lending huge amounts. They operate behind funds, banks, and diverse financial screens, but the money yielded by interest mechanically converges toward the very big lenders. You should notice that at no point did I mention any entrepreneurial spirit in these families. There was no mention, either, of potential companies that they would own and which could offer profitable, even very profitable, services or products and which could be said to be job providers for the people. No, I am talking to you only about persons of private means who have been storing up interest for centuries without doing anything useful."

"So you accumulate banknotes from generation to generation, is that what you are telling me? But everybody knows that money loses its value with the passing of time. And the world continues turning!" Anne had the sudden pleasant feeling of scoring a point.

"Yes, paper money loses its value because the central banks desperately try to adjust the quantity of money in circulation. Without entering into useless, technical details, know that by adjusting the short-term interest rate, they try to regulate the quantity of money in the commercial banks, which act as the multipliers of money. More money circulating means that prices increase and the currency loses its value of exchange with time. And, apparently, the economy seems to grow."

"I know almost nothing of financial matters, but I thought that the economy was following natural cycles, with highs and lows, like the seasons and the tides."

Her unknown host suddenly stood up and, despite the pain he obviously felt, was now making big steps, firmly leaning on his cane. "Nonsense! The cycles of creation follow a principle of complementarities. When it is winter in our hemisphere, it is summer in the other; each season is needed in order to facilitate the exchanges. There is no such thing for economic cycles. Why should humanity experience periods of prosperity followed by terrible crises? These two steps are not complementary; they are completely opposed. There is no need whatsoever to first experience misery and then discover wealth. These last years we have gone through a period of unprecedented monetary creation, which gave the illusion of economic growth and which gave birth to the stock exchange and real estate 'bubbles' all over the world. All of these rocketing prices simply indicate that a huge mass of money has been created by the banks in the form of debts. The central banks are behind this creation. Then, fearing these bubbles, they closed the money taps. This sudden scarcity of money made the bubbles explode. These excesses of debt are the origin of the crisis that we shall experience. I know that since we have triggered it."

They were face to face and were now looking into each other's eyes. Anne saw a deep sadness in this look. There was a long moment of silence; a thin connection seemed to weave between them.

"My family will not lose one franc, this is for sure. The opposite will be true. We are very closely involved in the decisions and actions of the major banks. We know beforehand the evolution of the money supply, and for centuries we have been regularly converting a great part of the paper money that we receive in the form of interest. We exchange them against tangible assets such as precious metals, land, real estate, oil, or the military-industrial complex. We act through different companies all over the world, and our possessions are as fabulous as they are discrete. Once again, we shall seize the properties of those who cannot repay us, and we shall rent them or sell them off later. The oligarchic families will make huge profits with the crisis, not to mention the fact that crises allow us to further our other agendas."

Anne was more and more disturbed. A quote came back to her: "Who controls the food supply controls the people; who controls energy can control whole continents; who controls money can control the world." If she remembered correctly, these words were reportedly a statement of Henry Kissinger. Aloud, she asked, "And no one protests?"

"We managed to stifle and marginalize the opinions of a few Austrian economists who had clearly perceived the dangers of the system of central banks and could have denounced it. Moreover, we took care that religions ignore the divine commandments in relation to interest-bearing loans. Only some Muslims resist us to some degree on this point in some countries."

"I confess that the biblical and Koranic quotes have disturbed me. But I did understand the mechanism 'there is overheating when there is too much money; and then, when there is too little, this generates a crisis.' But the central banks and paper money did not exist in the biblical times of Ezekiel. My question is, then, is there something else intrinsically fraudulent about loans with interest?"

"I rejoice to see that you have understood me! Even at the time of the prophets of the Old Testament, God knew very well that the mechanism of interest would ultimately result in the concentration of power in the hands of a small minority of people and that these powerful people could be tempted to follow the forces of evil. But you are right; this is probably not the only reason. From an external point of view, it seems that all things exist as distinct entities. But, as they were created by God, whose nature is harmonized, these things are naturally created to exist, grow, and multiply only through interdependent and harmonious relationships. An ideal relationship is established through a give-and-take action where the entity that initiates the relationship is giving to the other part, which accepts and receives and then gives something back in return to the initiator."

"You mean that exchange is naturally at the core of the economy?"

"Absolutely! You see, money is a simple tool aimed at facilitating exchanges. When I exchange with you item A for item B, it is obvious that from my point of view, your item B has more value than my item A. On your side, you think that A has more value than B. Both of us are thus satisfied. But imagine that I ask you to give me two apples for one apple in return. Would you accept that? No, of course you would not! With money, however, it looks normal. If I lend you one hundred francs, at a compound rate of 4%, in twenty years you will give me back at least two hundred. Are we not in an obsolete situation?"

"Then what can we do?"

"Observe the profound wisdom of the Koranic quote, 'Allah allows selling, but prohibits usury.' According to the major religions, ever since the founding of the world, humanity has been divided into two families. The first one was closer to God's will, whereas the other was further away from God's will. Cain murdered his brother, didn't he? This division also exists in finance. As you know, there are two distinct ways to invest. The first consists in buying shares, or pieces, of a company. When this company is thriving, it can share its profits with its shareholders as dividends. There are neither debts nor interest but a sharing of the simple fruits of the commercial gains. Whereas, when you buy bonds, there is bound to be a payment with interest—whatever the results. You can easily understand that bonds connected to debt go against the divine will. I just want to show you the difference between these two forms of investment, and I am not speaking of the imbalance that may exist between the shareholders and the employees of a company."

"The solution, therefore, would be to prohibit debt and bonds and create no more money? But that is impossible! Population is increasing. Countries have increasingly greater needs and thus need more and more money!" Anne suddenly felt that this discussion was leading nowhere. Confident in herself and in her pragmatism, she had the feeling that the old man was raving.

But he kept cold-bloodily developing his arguments. "What would happen if the monetary mass were constant and debts with interest were suddenly prohibited? It would be the end of the world—this is what you think, right? I can see that you wonder if I am sane, and you are forgiven. You should know that those who advocate banning debt and who could, in this way, seriously jeopardize the power of the oligarchic families like mine have, of course, no access to the major media to defend their point of view. Now let us reflect peacefully, if you can bear with and listen to me for a while without being impatient. Let us imagine an isolated island, without any bank on its territory. The population would not use credit but would use gold coins to make exchanges easier. If we were to believe you, after a few generations this population would be extinct. Surely not! As the population grew, the coins would have to be distributed among a greater number of hands, wouldn't they? They would thus become more and more rare. Do you still follow me? Their exchange value would increase and the price of the goods and of the services would tend to decrease regularly on this paradise island, unlike in our situation, where we see the prices soaring year after year."

"But then wouldn't people be inclined to postpone their purchases?"

"Right now, people do not hurry to buy in order to avoid these price increases. Likewise, when prices slowly decrease with the passing years, people wouldn't indefinitely postpone their purchases to benefit from it. On this miraculous island, after a few generations, the exchange value of the coins would become so strong that people would simply cut them in two or three in order to have smaller denominations. And in order to finance projects, these island people would either save money or invest in shares. When you borrow, you buy immediately and you pay later; when you save, you do the opposite. It is tempting to buy on credit, but when you have to pay with your savings, you think more about it, don't you think so?"

Before Anne could respond, he continued. "I am going to give you proof that this is not a theory. In the year 325, Emperor Constantine made some historical decisions: Byzantium was given the new name of Constantinople and became the capital of the empire, Christianity became the state religion, and a new currency was created. This gold coin, named the solidus, was a copy of the Greek drachma. From that moment, bankers had to monitor one another and swear that they would not dilute the composition of the solidus; otherwise, their hands would be amputated. Moreover, realizing that debts with interest had played a crucial role in the collapse of Rome, they were banned in application of the biblical principle. At that time, a stable currency and an absence of debts quickly resulted in tangible benefits and there was an unprecedented economic boom. Gold became central, commerce was thriving, and the state and the church became incredibly rich. A few examples of this fabulous era can still be seen in Ravenna and Istanbul."

The accumulation of this financial and mystical data could make one dizzy. If one were to believe all these statements, humanity would just have to obey the divine commandments and that would be enough for the fortune of the oligarchic families to be irremediably dissolved. It was dreamlike Anne thought.

The old man continued: "You want to defeat us? Abolish loans with interest and don't create any more money. Economic cycles will disappear, wealth will no longer be concentrated in the hands of a few mega creditors like me, and money will gain value with time. What you bequeath to your children will have more value than when you first got it. This is what I want you to explain in the book you are going to write." As he pronounced these last sentences, his voice was tense with a mystical passion.

Looking at Anne, he asked, "Do you understand at last why God has formally prohibited the interest-bearing loan? This is very simply to avoid the concentration of wealth and power in the hands of a few families. Otherwise, the spiritual entities revolting against God would use these same families and would maintain hell on earth, thus preventing mankind from rising to a divine level in order to create a better world. And that is precisely what is going on."

Anne was listening to him and thinking of the explanations given by her brother. Everything matched, but things were probably not as simple as that. "Why do you reveal all these things to me?"

"I already told you, I want you to write a book in order to explain things to the whole world. People have to know!"

"Why don't you do it yourself? Your fortune would pave the way and would eradicate any obstacle."

"First of all, if I appeared to be the author of such a book, I would probably be locked up as senile even before the first buyer could appear. And also, I need someone like you, who is living a normal life; you will be my adviser about the best way to present my revelations. I am actually much too aloof from the people I would like to address. Finally, I want a qualified collaborator, a professional who is recognized for the authority of her works. And for your personal ethics, I shall do everything so that you may check the veracity of my statements, at least partially."

Anne's brain was boiling, making plans. The topic was indeed interesting. Better than that, it was extremely thrilling and had a humanistic significance that she appreciated. Celebrity, or even glory, was of little import for her, but during their very special encounter, she felt that she had been impacted by a grace that needed to be shared. From a practical point of view, the money placed in her account would open all doors, and trained as she was to interview the important people of this world, she felt qualified to faithfully render the contents.

"Anne! Are you daydreaming?"

"Yes, forgive me, I was a bit lost."

"I could see that. Now, my dear, I see myself under the obligation to reveal something far less inspiring, but I believe I know you enough to think that this is not going to slow down your impetus; we can talk of an impetus, can we not?"

"We can."

"Wonderful! Then I have a question, what do you think will be the reaction of the other oligarchic families? How will this book be received?"

"I had not given much thought to that!"

"You have to think about it. It won't be long before they react. As soon as the book is released, we should expect that, rather quickly, bookstores will be filled with similar books, littered with false information, of course, but which may somehow confuse our readers. I will explain to you later what the deep reasons are that prompted me to let you know all these revelations, but you should know that the others won't accept what will appear in their eyes as high treason. Quite likely, I won't be able to live beyond the publication of this book, but this is unimportant. Ever since you have been here, just beside me, I regret that I have offered you what is somehow a poisoned chalice."

"What do you mean?"

"I also hesitated for a long time on the choice of the amount of money I offered you. I know that this amount may seem enormous to you, but first it prompts you to believe me when I tell you that the reigning families have unimaginable powers. And then this money will help you to release this book worldwide and to have it translated in several languages. You will have to awaken people's attention to a reality that is far more obscure than what they can imagine. You will present this story in the form of a novel. And in order to avoid any legal proceedings that might block the publication of the book, you will never quote any name, neither mine nor of any other family."

"Since I don't even know one syllable of it, I could hardly quote your name. But you were talking of a poisoned chalice, why would it be so?"

"Quite certainly, Goldstein has already warned other members of the oligarchic families, but in order to gain time, I shall make them believe that you were hired in order to write and promote a book on our philanthropic works. Yes, in order to enhance our image, our appearances, we are, as Jesus would say, like a tomb—white on the surface and stinking and full of vermin inside. I shall pretend that due to my old age, I desire to leave a positive trace in the history books the dominated people read. However, I should warn you that this will not work very long. Of course, they were not happy that I refused to take part in the last ceremony." He had pronounced this last sentence as if he was talking to himself.

"Ceremony? I don't follow you. What kind of treason are you talking about? I cannot easily grasp your motivation."

"We shall talk about it during our next meeting, but for your security, we must be quick and very careful. I shall contact you very soon to tell you the place chosen for our next meeting. Meanwhile, start working to find the connecting thread of the novel, and I trust you."

"So, then, I shall not return to Venice? By the way, why did you choose this city for this first meeting? I am rather insensitive to the charm of the lagoon."

"Venice has long been a financial and commercial center. But above all, five hundred years ago, it was from here that the black Venetian nobility started to spread, and my family belongs to it. At that moment, its power started to build up. So I thought that the place was fit to lay down the foundations of our collaboration. But it is late; you should not miss your airplane."

With an exquisite courtesy, the old man accompanied her to the door. He took her hand in his hands and kept it there for a moment. His eyes were blurred, whether from tiredness or sadness, she could not tell. But she was moved.

*

On the return trip, she sorted out the unanswered questions, thought that she would need her brother, and wondered how she would report this surrealistic day to Hans without causing him to panic. She kept worrying the whole time but yielded to the desire to overlook the danger and to believe that it had more to do with the paranoia of an old man than with the reality of his life. In order to be fully involved in the exciting work awaiting her, she knew that it would be necessary to do away with her anxiety but was not sure she could. However, she wanted to be worthy of the trust placed in her, and her heart and mind had to be free and light. She made a particular effort to be peaceful, breathed deeply, and napped for a while.

It was when she drove in the direction of Basel that an important part of this reality came back to her memory and struck her with violence. She had accepted a sum of four hundred million francs! Even if the man was immensely rich, he had not offered this present without expecting something in return, and the trip to Venice was undoubtedly the very beginning of servitude so extensive that it suddenly became frightening.

She was now becoming aware of her own thoughtless behavior! Of course, she would have to pay for the translators and the printing and distribution of the book, but the amount on her account was far above the expected expenses. She had the impression that she at last understood what she had just done, and she was afraid.

She also feared the reaction of Hans. He was a man totally deprived of frivolity, of absent-mindedness, and of any type of reaction one might label as immature, but he would become angry, no doubt. Already she could hear him ordering her to go and give this money back immediately. More than that, he would insist on going himself; yes, he would do just that.

Anne was sweating. They would sometimes argue, but they would never do so in front of Nicolas, and the topics were generally not so important. Only the complex relationship between Hans and John could entail more tension since Anne had a strong attachment to her brother. And finally, their delicious reconciliations might have served as an appetizer, when seen from a viewpoint of tender perversity. Unfortunately, in this case, she expected the worst. As she entered the city, she had made her decision. In order to make her commitment very clear, she would talk about money to her husband, but she would talk about a smaller amount of forty thousand francs. She could thus assert that she had already been remunerated and that her involvement in the project was no longer to be questioned.

*

It was late when she entered the apartment, and she had hardly closed the door when Nicolas jumped into her arms. "Mummy! Where have you been? You did not tell me that you were going on a trip!"

"Honey, this morning I did not know it, and it was just a small trip. Why are you not in bed yet?"

Hans was standing in the doorway. "He pretended to not be able to go to sleep before you came back."

"All right, enough is enough, little sweetheart! Come on, then, I shall tuck you in, and I want to hear you snore within three minutes!" Anne took Nicolas in her arms and climbed up the few steps leading to the mezzanine.

When she was back downstairs, Hans was attentively looking at her. "Are you hungry?"

"No, thank you, darling, dinner was served on the airplane."

"Come on and sit beside me and tell me the whole story from the beginning."

Hans was obviously worried, and Anne thought in a flash that, for the first time ever since they had known each other, she was about to tell him a lie. She felt uneasy, and that might show up.

"From the beginning?"

"Yes, because this story, which started out as fascinating, is becoming worrisome and I want to be informed."

"All right. Everything started with this letter. We thought it was a hoax, but it is not. It emanates from an important figure in the financial world who wants me to write a book. It will be his memoirs, so to speak. And the sum of money put on the account in my name at Goldstein's is part of my wages paid in advance."

"How much was put on the account?"

"Forty thousand francs."

"Forty thousand francs! Have you ever received such an amount to write a book, Anne?"

"No...Well, yes, when the book sold very well and I had some commission on the sales."

"But that was very rare, and I can't remember that you were paid in advance."

"That's true, but in this case, you see, I already had to travel and I will have to travel more for sure. There will be expenses. Moreover, I also need to have the book translated as well."

"Hmm... So, then, for you, this is all perfectly normal?"

"I didn't say that. I confess that this gentleman has strange ways of doing things, but I see behind his manners the fact that he is incredibly rich and thus used to seeing that everything is done according to his will. Moreover, he is very old."

"Ah, I see. He has the obsessions of an old man. And what is the name of this generous old chap?"

"Well, I don't know; he introduces himself as the unknown superior."

"What? You don't even know for whom you are working?"

"For the moment, he somehow prefers to remain anonymous. He simply told me that he belonged to one of the oligarchic families, the most important in the world."

Hans had become pale, had suddenly stood up, and was now pacing back and forth in the living room. "My darling, you are an intelligent woman, sensible and perfectly righteous, so I always trusted you completely and unconditionally even if, on a few occasions, I saw you commit yourself somewhat casually. But here I can no longer understand you. This story is not clear. I do not understand why you don't see it. Think about it! You receive a letter from Russia, which is incoherent, don't you think? Then, without your lifting a finger, an account is opened for you in a bank which is not yours and a pretty good sum of money is wired to it. And then you are asked—and that word is mild—to make a flying visit to Venice, four hundred miles from here, in order to meet this man who does not even introduce himself!"

Anne, crestfallen, was obliged to admit that she had been acting without thinking, but as she was firmly determined to see this adventure through to the end and tried to calm him down. "Listen, I understand your worries, and I propose that we ask John's advice. For once, his conspiratorial tendencies will be useful. If there is a danger, he will tell us and I shall see where I stand. But I would also like you to understand that this work represents a professional opportunity for me."

"All right, call John. Call him right now." Hans came closer to his wife and took her in his arms. "Once again, darling, it is not you whom I don't trust, you know that. Forgive me if I challenge you, but this is the first time that your professional life has led you into such adventures."

"You are right, I shall call John." Her call reached her brother's voicemail, however. "John, would you please call me back as soon as you hear this message? This is about the letter from Russia, which you surely remember. I am being offered a job that makes Hans worry, and me too a little, I should confess."

*

Karl "X" was thinking, leaning back on the imperial armchair adorning his no-less-imperial office, when his secretary came in. "It is a call for you, sir. Are you available?"

"Who is calling?"

"Mr. Robert 'Y.'"

"Yes, I'll take the call," he said, waiting until the secretary left the room before picking up his extension. "My dear Bob, how are you doing?"

"All right, all right, as well as possible for a person of my age. And you?"

"Like a young man!"

"I know. You are a stripling compared to me; you don't need to insist on this point. Actually, I have a reason for calling you. I have been toying for quite some time with a project I have just started, and I would like to tell you about it—though our friend Goldstein has surely already talked to you about it."

Not waiting for Karl's answer, he continued. "As we all think, the hour has come to denounce the false beliefs and to let the world know the truth. Of course, the media has been doing their job through numerous scenarios, but nevertheless, our actions have remained out of sight. I have, therefore, decided to release a book that will reveal our good deeds. It is high time that mankind opens its eyes on this global lie, don't you think?"

"Of course, of course. But how will you proceed?"

"In the most simple way. I have found a ghostwriter. It's a journalist, a young woman who is very charming, by the way. She already has a record of several well-written biographies, and she is available. I have already met her."

"Ah! You did not waste time!"

"At my age, dear friend, determination is one of the only resources remaining in my possession. I wired a good amount of money—reasonable for us but a good incentive for her to agree. Zeros always make a powerful impact. I met her in Venice, by the way."

"In Venice?"

"Yes. I insisted that she see me in the appropriate setting so that she will value the importance of the mission that I have given her. I am also contemplating inviting her to the coming ceremony. I feel that she is very much in support of our ideas, but the meeting will not fail to convince her for good. I am certain to have made the right choice, and, should it not work properly, we still have the option that applies in those cases. Her name is Anne Standfort. She is married, but her husband is insignificant. And, like everybody, she loves money. Don't worry, I control her."

There was a moment of silence, which probably meant different things to each of them. Karl broke the silence after a sigh. "Well, my dear friend, my best wishes are with you, but before I leave you, it is my duty to tell you how disappointed the great master was at your absence at the last ceremony. He expressed it forcefully. As for me, I was holding a present I wanted to give him on behalf of us all. It is a unique present, coming from Korea, and is one more token of our untiring fidelity. However, for this present to display all its value, we had to be united and your absence made the thing impossible. I was not the only one to feel regret."

"I know, I know. Believe me, I was also very embarrassed. However, you know the illnesses that affect me and my difficulties of mobility. The doctors prescribed that I should avoid any journey. Today I can thank them for being so adamant. I feel a bit better, and I shall attend the next ceremony."

"Well, accept the oracle, my friend. You know how much our great master loves us and counts on us."

He put down the receiver and leaned his head back on the armchair. An uncomfortable sensation had taken hold of him. He had known Bob for a long time. He was part of the clan, was tied to it, but had never manifested any philanthropic or altruistic will in its favor. He took advantage of it, of course, and that was all. And suddenly, he wanted to be the spokesman of their common cause? He wanted to divulge the work of their master? Why not evangelize the globe? This smelled fishy, and Karl had a sensitive nose. He sought a number in his address book and called. A familiar voice answered, "Yes, I am listening."

"Where are you now?"

"I am in Paris, going back to Seoul by the first plane."

"The program has changed. Take the first flight to Basel. Your colleagues from the former East German secret services will be waiting for you. You will recognize them?"

"Of course. It was not long ago when we were working for—"

"Yes, yes. No need to go into details."

"All right. What's the job description, then?"

"For the moment, you have to find the address of a certain Anne Standfort, journalist. She must be living downtown in Basel. Enter her house and take care of her computer. Business as usual. I want to know everything. And then follow her wherever she goes and report to me whatever you see and hear. Will you be equipped?"

"Of course. Nothing else?"

"We shall see if the situation requires more motion."

"How long will that be?"

"I shall let you know in due time." With that, he hung up, certain that he would be scrupulously obeyed.

Chapter 4

The next morning, John had not yet called. Anne tried again, left a new message insisting that it was urgent, and then sat at her computer and started doing research. Not knowing where to go, she typed "debt money" and a succession of sites appeared on her screen, confirming the stories of the old man: the Bilderberg meetings, instances where only the university professors supporting the "new ideas" were able to publish their works, and so forth. She was astounded. She was also worried that her brother hadn't phoned back, and she made the very feminine decision to take a break for a few hours, relax, and go out.

After one hour, she had had enough of walking and returned home, determined to keep searching on the web. When she entered the hall, a strange smell tickled her nostrils. It smelled like tobacco but something sweeter as well. She decided to change the flowers' water. They really needed it, especially the fragile lilies.

She resumed her investigation by researching the reigning families connected to the black nobility and found a huge number of websites. It was not easy to find out which ones could be taken seriously. She took out all those that looked questionable, and she noticed that the topic was very popular on the Internet. Almost all the contributors agreed that important decisions were made far away from national parliaments. The less militant websites stated that world affairs were decided under the influence of powerful lobbies, more or less visible, without mentioning a particular role for reigning families. The most radical websites went as far as to state that the world was controlled by diverse secret societies, themselves controlled by a few very powerful oligarchic families. According to these sites these families were not always on good terms among themselves, but they had a common objective: to see the emergence of a more global world in which power would be centralized in a minimum number of hands. This would allow the families to rule from the background even more easily. Some secret societies would be used as bridges to organizations visible to the general public in order to coordinate the implementation of their worldview.

Money would be, of course, the driving force. An "objective" would be set, and money would follow a certain direction, also carefully set up. "To summarize: secret societies, strategic places, largesse toward the families, centralized decision-making from which the main ideas would come which were to radiate outward, the assemblage looked perfect".

Anne remembered the words of Aldous Huxley: "It is perfectly possible for a man to be out of prison, and yet not free; to be under no physical constraint and yet to be a psychological captive, compelled to think, feel, and act as representatives of the national state, or of some private interest within the nation, want him to think, feel, and act.... The nature of psychological compulsion is such that those who act under constraint remain under the impression that they are acting on their own initiative. The victim of mind-manipulation does not know that he is a victim. To him the walls of his prison are invisible, and he believes himself to be free. That he is not free is apparent only to other people. His servitude is strictly objective."

She thought about what Huxley wrote: a world religion, a world government, a world currency issued by a world bank, and crowning this beautiful vision of the world, the establishment of eugenics. Anne switched off the computer. She was cold.

Just then, the telephone rang; it was John. "Anne, where are you?"

"I'm at home, but where have *you* been? I have been waiting for your call since yesterday."

"I forgot my phone at a friend's house. I just got it back and listened to your message. What's going on?"

"Do you remember the letter I received from Russia, from the man who called himself the unknown superior? He wants me to write a book on him. I went to see him in Venice."

"In Venice? He had you go to Venice?"

"Yes, I shall explain everything to you. But Hans is worried, and we would like you to give us your opinion. Can you come?"

"It's not possible for me to come there, but you can come here. Things are actually falling into place. Jump in your car and join me in Ingolstadt, in Germany."

"Ingolstadt? You're crazy!"

"I am not at all crazy, Anne. Do as I say. If Hans is willing to ask me questions, it is because he is really worried, and he is right to be. Travel light, just a small piece of luggage. I shall reserve a room at the Hotel Rappensberger. It takes four hours by car, so you should be here by eight o'clock tonight. I will be waiting for you, and say thanks to Hans for being willing to consult me. It is no doubt a good decision."

Anne just had time to tell Hans that he would have to look after Nicolas. Because there was no school on Wednesday afternoon, he was at a friend's house; however, she knew that he would surely complain. Quite disturbed, she thought of all the worries which had accumulated since the arrival of that letter! She would have liked to turn back time. Three days ago, her only concern in life was the difficult relationship between her husband and her brother. Today, everything seemed to make them closer, but at what price?

    She prepared her toothbrush and toiletries and some clean clothes, put everything in a travel bag, and began her trip to Ingolstadt. Unaware to her, a metallic gray sedan smoothly pulled out onto the road thirty yards behind her old Volkswagen.

*

Shin Jon Gol was satisfied. He found inactivity to be a waste of time, and the words *rest* and *holiday* were not part of his vocabulary. He immediately got to work, and one hour later he was in possession of all the information he needed, including a recent picture of Anne, her son, and her husband. He only had to change his sky-blue sportswear for a formal suit and his sneakers for flexible loafers, and go to the airport. He was completely self-confident, never doubted his talents, and never questioned the justification of his deeds. Because of this, the conviction of being under the protection of some sort of divine presence was a guarantee for the success of all his undertakings, and he would progress in life with the steady pace of the one who meets no resistance.

    In a few hours he was in Basel, where he met his two associates. He showed them the pictures and gave them the basic information. Part of the job was to hack into the computer so that all the keystrokes could be transmitted to those interested. The apartment had to be searched in order to find anything of interest, and Anne had to be tailed for an undetermined period. Who would do what would become clearer as the days went by. This work was all too simple. Without expressing it, he hoped that things would become heated. The whole business lacked a bit of spice.

    When they arrived in front of the building, Anne was leaving, walking nonchalantly. The weather was mild. He noticed, however, that she was not wearing a coat, which meant that she would not be away for long. Shin ordered one of the two men to come with him while the other stayed outside to watch for Anne and inform him when she came back. He would personally check the computer. Ten minutes were enough. He decided not to start the search of the apartment. Without knowing exactly why, he felt that she would be back very soon, and his intuition was never mistaken. Hardly one hour had passed when she returned, still walking casually.

There was nothing to do but wait. Meanwhile, they took their positions at a good distance from one another. In case of an emergency, Shin and his accomplice would jump into their car, parked at the angle to the street; the other would remain in place and start searching.

Fortunately, they did not have to wait very long. Anne was out again, this time with a light coat and a travel bag, which she threw in a Volkswagen parked in front of the door. Shin moved off a few seconds after her. The tank was full; he could cover a distance of about 350 miles. Keeping a reasonable distance, he saw her heading for the outskirts of the city. He inserted a CD of Oriental music in the CD player and let the road peacefully unwind its ribbon. Wherever she was going, he would be there, very close to her, and he felt exhilarated at the thought that this woman, about whom he knew nothing and around whom he was weaving a web without feeling any remorse, would not escape him. He did not care whether she was guilty of anything wrong or an innocent victim. He was totally happy when the task was accomplished according to the given instructions. He would not burden himself with any other consideration. His colleague had fallen asleep.

*

Karl had not left his office all day, and he was unhappy. He had the impression that he had done nothing concrete, the same thought turning in his mind like a panicked insect that fears the light and yet approaches it. Wanting to discover the truth, he called Bob.

After exchanging pleasantries, Karl introduced the reason for his call. "I wanted to let you know that the more I think of your project, the more I like it. You can count on me to give you support if necessary. And, to make things easier for you, I have already sent one of our best supervisors to Basel. He has spotted the comings and goings of the young lady. A simple call from your side will be enough for me to use one or the other of our plans. This fellow is fearful and quick, and his efficiency is unmatched. In brief, until the end of the operation, you have my full support."

"Ah, very good, very good! It's only within our circles that such professionalism can be assured, isn't it? I truly thank you and shall keep you informed."

"You are welcome. It is my pleasure."

Karl put the receiver down. He must have been mistaken. Was he becoming paranoid with time?

Bob's voice was natural and the affair would develop without complications. Even so, according to Shin, the woman was very pretty. It would be necessary to prevent this silly old guy from having his head turned.

*

As John had predicted, Anne entered the city of Ingolstadt at about eight o'clock. She had no problem finding the Hotel Rappensberger, a gorgeous five-star hotel, and when she parked her car in the parking lot, she could see John in the entrance, waiting for her.

"Here you are at last!" John kissed her warmly. "You look tired."

"There are reasons for that. I have been like a spinning top these last few days."

"Come in. We shall have dinner, and you will tell me everything."

The luxury of the place was a surprise for Anne. This splendor was not in her brother's habits, and he understood her question before she asked.

"Yes, I know, this is not the kind of place I usually go to, but I wanted to offer you a treat, especially since it is our first getaway since our teenage years. On top of that, the situation we are in is not normal!"

"You're right."

"Let's sit here," John said, motioning to a nearby table. "We can talk peacefully. There's a good distance between tables."

They sat down after a nod of approval from the head waiter and took time to focus on the menu. Anne hesitated, not having much appetite.

"I suggest the lobster cooked in court bouillon. It is their specialty."

"Lobster?"

"You don't like that?"

"Yes, I do, of course, but it's not my daily fare."

"That's one good reason to try it! And what about a Pouilly Fumé to go with it? I am not sure it's the right wine for lobster but I leave it up to you."

"Tell me, are we celebrating today?"

"Pouilly Fumé is your favorite wine, isn't it?"

"I am delighted that you remember that."

"You see! Since the future is uncertain, let us enjoy the present," he said, calling the waiter over.

*

A few tables away, two men had just started to have their dinner. One was an Oriental man in his thirties. The other was extremely pale and looked sleepy. Their rather unusual attitude went unnoticed in the dining room. Indeed, either they were worried, or they had just had an argument. They both had gloomy faces, and they did not exchange even one word during the whole meal. Anne and John had not paid any attention to them.

*

It was well past midnight when Anne and John went back to their rooms. She had explained all the details of the recent events, starting again from the beginning. John expressed a very strong annoyance when she announced the sum put in the numbered account and did not hide his opinion. "Why didn't you call me before putting your signature on those documents? Did you at least read them?"

"I skimmed over the main points. It was nothing but the opening of an account."

"Yes, but look at the amount, Anne, look at the amount! You put yourself squarely under his control!"

"You're right. I don't know what I was thinking. I was not attracted by the money, you must believe me. No doubt it is the oddness of the whole affair that fascinated me."

"Forgive me for saying it so bluntly, but you have acted unconscionably. I can only hope that nothing other than the writing of this book will be asked of you, but I should confess that I have doubt that is the case. Even Hans would have been a good adviser! What did he say when you told him this crazy story? I assume that his reaction was just as negative as mine?"

"I lied and told him the present was just forty thousand francs."

"This is getting better and better!"

"But why should we see danger absolutely everywhere? It's just a crazy old man, nothing more than that. I shall write his book, people will talk about him, that will make him satisfied and that is all."

"I would like to believe you, dear sister. Unfortunately, the odds of this old man being crazy, as you claim him to be, are unlikely. That hypothesis would be by far the more reassuring. I suggest that we go to bed; we need a good night's rest. Tomorrow, I have things to teach you, and it just so happens that in the very city where we are now, I can give you proof of what I am saying."

They made plans to meet again for breakfast and then go to John's room, which had a small living room where they could talk discretely. Though Anne felt the secrecy was unnecessary, she agreed.

*

The next morning, after an enormous breakfast, they went back to John's room, as they had planned. He was so busy with all the things he had to tell to his sister that he did not notice a light tobacco smell floating in the air. Without any reservations, he started to talk of the situation. "I really believe that you were trapped and that you will serve as bait. With such partners, you will not be without danger."

"But what would their goal be?"

"You see, even if this man would like to redeem himself at the end of his life and let the world discover a colossal truth capable of completely changing the course of history, do you believe that his clan will let him do as he wants with no reaction?"

"He told me that he would not outlive this adventure, but I thought he was raving."

"He was certainly not raving, but the point where I am blocked is the reason for his choice. Why did he choose you?"

"He told me that he had enjoyed the biographies I had written."

"It makes sense, but it is not enough for me. Do you remember our conversation with Nicolas?"

"How can I forget? I was amazed at how interested he was by your speech. At first I thought that he would send you packing with your stories, but no, he wanted more. And he is just twelve years old! I must confess that I was more worried by this aspect of the conversation than by the contents of your speech. Having said that, in Venice the unknown superior told me that he would give me more information during our next meeting."

"Where is this next meeting scheduled?"

"I don't know yet."

"You must realize how serious your accepting this money is. You are not dealing with just any ordinary person, Anne. These people have always been ready to do anything in order to reach the goal they have set."

"But what goal are you talking about?" Though she completely trusted her brother, Anne could not refrain from feeling a little bit upset.

"Their goal is nothing less than world order! This is the only thing they want, the only thing they work for. The world order means that they will control the world. Do you understand?"

"What I don't understand is where I fit in all this."

"I don't understand it either, and this is why I am so worried. I fear that you are but a tiny pawn on a giant chess game and that you will be crushed by machinery about which you know nothing. This is an impressive organization. To help you understand, imagine an onion."

"An onion?"

"Yes, you will see the comparison is relevant. The outer skin is what you read in the media. This is the story fed to the people of modest means, like you and me. Just below this level, the lobbyists are working on groups and politicians. Then, underneath, you find the Bilderberg and the Council on Foreign Relations. Digging even more deeply, you arrive at the Trilateral Commission. If you go down one more step, you stand face to face with less visible societies and certain Masonic lodges. And the exploration reaches the bottom with the Luciferian societies and the famous families at the heart of the system, where pure information is not yet distorted. You have to realize that this octopus has been active for several centuries. In 1776, Adam Weishaupt created the Bavarian Illuminati, often called simply the Illuminati. The seal of the Illuminati is found on the US one-dollar banknote! Some of their other symbols are there too, for example, the eye of Horus, or the eye in the triangle, which is the Luciferian symbol."

"You mean to say that the world order means Luciferian beliefs?"

"What about Halloween? What is it?"

"A celebration for children."

"Yes, of course, any means will do to infiltrate. These people can be found in Masonic lodges and later in the universities, where they train brilliant people who will be put in key positions. Thus, for instance, most economists will tell you that central banks are a good thing; those who disagree have been banned from universities for quite a time."

"I don't understand you any more, John. You are talking nonsense, and you frighten me!"

"I do want to frighten you. Excuse me if I am not clear enough, but this whole story irritates me so much that I am losing my mind. You have to be extremely careful."

"I don't know what to do anymore, John. I cannot really say no."

"No, you are right. Moreover, we should not show that we are worried. They would be on their guard. On our side, we should not lower our guard. For the moment, it is the best thing we can do. What you need to do, Anne, is to be able to spot them."

"To spot them?"

"Yes, Anne. Your old lunatic may not be acting alone, so I shall give you a lot of information. For instance, they can be identified by the particular way that they have to shake hands, and they have several other distinct signs. I'll explain all this in more detail in my e-mails. No, I cannot send you anything, and surely not by e-mail."

"Why?"

"Because your computer is more than likely already hacked."

"You're really exaggerating."

"Hardly. I know what I am talking about." John was now striding up and down the room nervously. Suddenly he stopped in front of Anne. "Put on your coat, we're going out. I am going to show you something."

"All right. What are you going to show me?"

"It's the proof of what I was talking about, the proof of the existence of the Illuminati. Adam Weishaupt was a professor of theology at Ingolstadt University. On May 1, 1776, he founded his secret society, the Bavarian Illuminati. I shall show you the commemorative plaque, which still exists. You will therefore see the place where he organized the gatherings of the Illuminati."

"Well, if you believe that it is useful."

"Yes, I believe so. And then we shall go back to Basel together. I shall try, without frightening your husband, to stick to you like a leech."

"But, John, what about your business?"

"That will wait, Anne. Even if it is not the time to let go of the reins, it will wait."

"Thank you, John!"

"All right, come on. Put on a scarf; it seems that the wind has started blowing."

They went out. After a short distance, John turned around several times as discretely as possible. The street was deserted. Very quickly they arrived at the corner of the Theresienstrasse and John showed the commemorative plaque to Anne. They went around the building, which was in bad shape.

"You see, the sect of the Bavarian Illuminati really existed. There is a wealth of literature on the subject, but most of the time it remains quite far from the reality. Weishaupt's Illuminism is essentially the philosophy from which the concept of the new world order was born, and the ultimate goal is to concentrate the wealth and the power in the hands of some major sages. Weishaupt mostly focused on elaborating the idea that in order to improve the world, revolutions have to be kindled by creating conflict between opposing ideas. Progress does not come through cooperation but through endless struggle. This was the start of the Hegelian dialectics and its thesis/antithesis/synthesis theories fifty years later. According to this philosophy, in order to establish the essential human rights of equality and liberty, it was first of all necessary to destroy all religion and all civil society and to abolish private property. He wanted to establish a godless religion, based on reason, morality, and ecology. The ultimate goal was to make all mankind one body under the rule of the unknown superiors. Now you understand why I took so seriously that letter you received?"

"Yes, I do."

"I thought it would be good to show you this commemorative plaque to give you proof that the idea of a new world order has been here for a few centuries. Illuminism had a strong influence on freemasonry at that time, all over the world as well as in universities and the sciences. In particular, Weishaupt had a powerful impact on Robespierre, Mirabeau, Voltaire, and Philippe of Orléans. I do not wish to bore you with historical details, but at least you should know that the French Revolution was inspired by Illuminism, particularly the violent religious persecutions, such as those in Vendée, as well as the establishment of the Terror and of the Cult of the Supreme Being."

"How can you be sure about all that?"

"It seems that Weishaupt received powerful financial support at that time, and it helped Illuminism to thrive. But in 1786, the Bavarian police crushed Illuminism and published many texts written by Weishaupt. As an anecdote, you should know it is no coincidence that the date on the Masonic pyramid featured on the US one-dollar banknote is 1776. Next to it, you have the motto 'Novus Ordo Seculorum.'"

"I thought the date represented the year of independence of the United States. But tell me about Weishaupt. What happened to him after 1786?"

"He continued secretly, but shortly before his death in 1822, filled with remorse, he returned to the Catholic Church."

Anne read the commemorative plaque and suddenly exclaimed, "Look! A synagogue was created here!"

"All right, let's go. It is already ten o'clock. We should pick up our luggage at the hotel. If the roads are not jammed, we shall be in Basel around three o'clock. Can you go without lunch?"

"With everything I gulped down this morning, I would be surprised to be hungry anytime soon."

"Good. You should call Hans."

"I already did that."

"And what did he say?"

"He is happy to know that I am with you."

"Dear boy! His brain is finally working!"

"John, you should not talk like that." Anne was smiling.

He took the wheel, and she sat down comfortably. Light music made her doze until Basel.
As soon as they arrived in the hall of Anne's home, John noticed a strange smell. "Is Hans smoking blond tobacco now?"

"He never smokes, you know that. Why do you ask?"

"There is a strange smell in your house."

"It must be the flower water. I noticed it earlier too."

"Where did you put these flowers?"

Anne looked around. There weren't any flowers. "Hans probably threw them out, but it was already late when he did so."

Anne was happy to be back home. She took her coat off and did not pay attention to her brother's scowl as he went to the computer.

"What is your password?"

"HAN18—HAN for Hans, Anne, and Nicolas and the eighteen for the day we met."

"You should change it. It is too easy to identify."

"There is nothing secret on my computer!" she replied, turning to go to the kitchen.

She was already busy preparing coffee when he called her. "Look at this. You've got a message."

"From whom?"

"From your old lunatic, apparently."

"And what does he say?"

"Come and see for yourself. It confirms all that I said about your new servitude."

Anne came closer with a cup of coffee, and they read together.

My dear Anne, I hope that you are doing well. As for myself I was very happy to get to know you. Our meeting confirmed that I made the right choice, and I am more than ever convinced that we shall do a very good job together.

The second step is waiting for us in the United States, at Elberton, Georgia. You will take the 6:17 a.m. KLM flight on Sunday, October 3 from Basel to Amsterdam, where you will arrive at 7:55 a.m. Then you will take a Delta flight at 10:45 a.m. and arrive in Atlanta at 2:35 p.m., local time. From there, you will rent a car for the two-hour drive to Elberton. I took the initiative to reserve a room for you at the Econo Lodge hotel. As for me, I shall see you on the fourth of October. I shall pick you up at your hotel around two o'clock in the afternoon.

Looking forward to seeing you soon. I wish you the best.

"You see, my little sister? You are now under the orders of this gentleman, and I have a clue about what he wants to show you. But we'll beat him at his own game! I will go with you. Do you have the phone number for reservations at the airport?"

"Yes, here it is."

John dialed the number, stated that he was calling on behalf of Anne Standfort, and reserved a second seat without any difficulty. The next thing was to inform Hans, which would not be the easiest part. However before she did so, hand in hand they went to pick up Nicolas at school. He was joking with his friends, but upon seeing John, he ran to him and jumped in his arms.

"Are you staying long?"

"Just for a day, my poppet, and the day after tomorrow, I shall kidnap your mother."

"Oh! Again?"

"You should give me a hug before moaning!"

Nicolas threw his arms around his mother's neck and they went home together, stopping briefly at the cake shop to buy Nicolas a huge strawberry ice cream sundae capped with whipped cream.

"Will you be away for long?"

"A few days, my darling, but it is for my work. And I know that when I am not here, Dad spoils you like mad. Isn't that so?"

"Yeah, but not every day."

"Come on, come on! You're cheating! Now, tell me, do have any homework?"

"Just a little."

"Then go quickly to your room and do what you have got to do. I would like you to go to bed early this evening."

John was peacefully looking through a magazine when, after only five minutes, the voice of Nicolas rang out. "Uncle John, would you come and see my drawings?"

As soon as his uncle had entered the room, Nicolas told him, "I have no drawing to show you, but I have something to tell you. The letter has disappeared."

"The letter? The letter from Russia?"

"Yes."

"Where did you put it?"

"In one of my desk drawers, just in front of you."

John was trying to hide his thoughts from Nicolas. Of course the apartment had been visited. The smell of tobacco was a clue, but he thought that only the computer had been hacked. Now there was no doubt, and the disappearance of the letter opened new fields of reflection. Was the author of the letter attempting to get it back? It was quite unlikely, even though the letter was compromising on several counts. More likely, other persons were interested in getting hold of the document, and this confirmed his concerns, even if he no longer needed the confirmation.

"You may have thrown it away without paying attention."

"No, I didn't! I am tidy, you know."

"Listen, this isn't very important. In any case, I shall be with your mother during her coming trips, and she will be protected. Do you trust me?"

"Yes."

"All right, then. You don't need to worry."

The evening with Hans was rather peaceful. He wasn't thrilled by this series of trips, but he was aware of the demands connected to his wife's profession. Once more, she would receive a very substantial remuneration, from which the whole family would benefit, so he made efforts to adopt a flexible attitude. Moreover, John would be with her, and this was extremely reassuring. Indeed, he who saw conspiracies everywhere would be super vigilant.

They made the most of the next day. While Anne went shopping and prepared the apartment so the housework would not be too complicated for Hans, John focused on reorganizing his schedule, postponing some appointments and cancelling others. This change of program would probably affect his work quite a lot. But the letter had disappeared, and this was a serious matter. Though he could not fully understand the implications, it made him realize more than ever the importance of his presence with Anne. On October 3, the sun had not yet risen and Nicolas was still sleeping when the taxi came to take them to the airport.

*

When Shin's colleague gave him the letter he had found in Nicolas's desk, more than a week had passed.

"You are giving me this only now?"

"You were not here."

"You should have called me. I would have told you what to do. Who's going to take the heat? It will be me, of course."

"How could I have known?"

"I know. That is why you have to keep me informed at all times."

"All right. You just have to say that I went there only yesterday."

"And what were you doing during the other days? Would you by any chance consider me a fool?"

"No, no."

"OK, shut up, then. That would be better."

"What will you do, then?"

"It is none of your business. I shall fix your mess, as usual."

Shin examined the letter and read it again. He did not notice anything special and thought that the boss could wait a few more days before being informed of its contents. He would probably get angry. But this would not be the first time, and it would surely not be the last.

Chapter 5

The temperature was particularly chilly this early gray morning, and Anne, shivering in her linen coat, regretted not dressing more warmly. They barely had time to swallow an insipid cup of tea at the airport, and she still felt like having a hot drink. John offered her the window seat, and in a few minutes, they were above the clouds. Whenever she was traveling and the aircraft reached the altitude where the sky was completely blue, Anne was invaded by a double sensation. She was filled with wonder, of course, but also with a muted anxiety—men try anything and challenge all the laws of nature, as if they were birds. But her brother did not seem to be in the mood for dreaming.

"Look, I have brought a few documents related to the September 11 attacks. I would like you to read them. They come from diverse professionals—engineers, architects, pilots, and the like—and they point out at long list of discrepancies and call for a more detailed investigation."

Anne repressed a sigh and started to read. According to the papers, the fire of the two towers could not have been strong enough to cause the fall of the buildings. No building with a steel structure had ever collapsed, even after far more violent fires. What, then, explained the sudden collapse of the towers, the like of which can be observed only in the case of controlled demolition? What explained the fact that Building Seven, located just nearby and into which no airplane had crashed, also collapsed, dropping like a stone? And this took place shortly after Mr. Silverstein had suggested that firemen "pull" the building? This well-informed Mr. Silverstein had been the owner of the two towers and of Building Seven for just two months and had had the extraordinary foresight of purchasing a substantial insurance policy against airplane crashes, an insurance which enabled him to pocket a huge amount of money. What explained that, according to a thermal map provided by NASA, the temperature of the rubble in the basements was far greater than that of the fusion of steel, if not that military explosives had been used? What explained the pictures of beams sheared off at forty-five-degree angles, just like in the case of controlled explosions? How could one believe the official version, which claimed that the passports of the terrorists had been miraculously found intact amid the thousands of tons of rubble at the feet of the towers?

In regard to flight A77, which had officially crashed on the Pentagon, why was the lawn not even burned, even though officially it was stated that the absence of significant debris and body parts were the result of a gasification following the intense heat at the time of the crash? And yet in 2003, when the *Columbia* shuttle had exploded at an altitude of 210,000 feet, debris and human parts had been found? According to John's document, it was the Global Hawk, an unmanned aerial vehicle similar to a small Boeing, which might have crashed on the Pentagon. The inconsistencies were listed page after page.

Anne was discouraged, and she closed the document. The gap between reality and the official version could make one dizzy. Could one still believe any authority? Was trust not turning into some form of guilty gullibility?

"Anne, tell me, what is a conspiracy if not some form of secret pact between several persons with the goal of fulfilling their agendas? Do you think that it is inconceivable?"

"No, of course not. There are reported cases of backstage manipulation."

"Then, you see, a person like me, who can build theories based upon wide but strong foundations in order to objectively examine all the divergent viewpoints, risks being labeled as a conspiracy nut, if not mentally ill."

"Is that your case?"

"Of course! The accusation is easy and classical. In that case, there is no debate. To claim to be skeptical by using the arguments of the official version only strengthens the latter. We are then dealing with a so-called skepticism, another name for obscurantism."

"Please admit, though, that some people can elaborate warped ideas. Remember the prophecies for the year 2000. Were not computers worldwide bound to explode on December 31 at midnight?"

"That's true. The famous skeptics use these inconsistencies to make a hodgepodge. It is an excellent strategy of disinformation. Try it for yourself. Spread some information on the Internet that is half true. And then insert among this something completely false but which can be checked in an irrefutable manner. Wait for a few days and then call an expert, who will denounce this element. You will then see that no one can distinguish what is true from what is false. The majority will be delighted to accept the version issued by an accepted authority."

"I read somewhere that one of the most amazing phenomenon's of our time is the impossibility to maintain a wall of secrecy around any activity whatsoever. It seems, then, that only active disinformation can keep the curious away. Yet is it not rather the number of participants that prevents from keeping an absolute confidentiality?"

"Conspiracies have been seen involving big groups—for instance, the Manhattan Project for the creation of the atomic bomb. But, in most cases, a small group of well-trained professionals is enough. When the tasks are well compartmentalized and each group has access only to limited information, security is better guaranteed. If a traitor appears, he and his family are threatened. Things are organized so that the person has no access to the media and the trick is played. In any case, the process of disinformation does the rest."

"Do you believe that these unknown superiors can pull the strings and remain in the shadows?"

"With the money and the influence which they have, there is no doubt about that."

In the case of September 11, it was important to immediately raise the most basic question anybody would ask—why—and then the question of who. Who benefits from the crime is the question in criminal affairs. Here the two questions could find their answer in a reality that is perhaps little known and yet quite likely—oil. As to who, the answer could also be detected. It would not be the first time that foes from the past or present made an alliance to serve their interests, and the interests generally have no other friends than money and power. In any case, one thing was certain: Following the attacks, many laws, such as the Patriot Act, were voted on with the goal of strongly and insidiously curbing individual freedoms. Who said that the end justifies the means? Anne could not remember at this precise moment, but the statement really fit many people, as well as many situations.

The flight attendant brought the tea she had ordered. As Anne turned away from John, she hit the tray. Drops of hot tea fell on her blouse.

"I am sorry, Madam. I am so sorry."

"It is my fault. There's no need to excuse yourself."

"I shall try to clean it with some water."

"No, I shall do that by myself."

"May I help you?"

"No, it's not necessary. It's not serious."

In the lavatory, the stain was easily washed out. Anne felt that the foul smell in that place was familiar to her, but because she was still thinking about what she had just heard, she didn't pay further attention to the incident. She went back to sit with John.

"Tell me, going back to what you were just saying, what leeway does the average person have in this kind of affair?"

"Your blouse is completely wet!"

"Nothing serious. Answer me. The everyday person, a guy like you, a girl like me—what can we do?"

"We can't do so much, I confess, but I personally don't like to be lied to, especially when I don't know."

"Because if you are informed, it is less painful?"

"It is hardly less painful, but in any case, I can no longer accept being taken for a potted plant."

"Your actions speak louder than your words, my little brother. Otherwise, what would you be doing here?"

"Yes, you are right, but if only there was only one September 11th! We have been manipulated for so many years! Conspiracy after conspiracy, coup d'état after coup d'état, sham attack after sham attack—everything is organized, covered up, and distorted. Whatever Hans thinks, conspiracy is everywhere and is permanent. Not to accept, to see, the reality is to cover it up, and this is serious."

"I don't follow you."

"If you start to doubt a counter-truth under the pretext that the initial truth was declared to be from a reliable source, you have no way to let the real truth show up."

"All right, but what can we do?"

"We have to search and scratch. This is what courageous people are doing and what they have discovered was helpful to cast a powerful doubt on so many official statements. Let's go back to September 11. Why do you think that most of the writers of the investigative commission denied their initial statements? Is it because they realized that they were lacking information, or rather because the conclusions were turning into a hoax?"

"I don't know, John, I don't know. I find it terrible to live with the thought that the people who govern us can lie over such serious matters."

"It has always been like this; for instance, have you heard of the declaration of war against Poland made by Hitler?"

"Yes, of course."

"Polish people supposedly attacked a German radio tower, thus forcing Hitler to retaliate."

"It's possible."

"But it is false. In reality, Hitler was searching for a justification for invading Poland and this attack was launched under his orders by Germans dressed in Polish uniforms. They attacked the transmitter of Gliwice to justify an attack. You did not know that?"

"No, I've never heard of it."

"What about the Vietnam War?"

"Yes, a colleague told me about a recent program where McNamara talked about this and called it a mistake. He said that they believed they were being attacked in the Gulf of Tonkin but that was completely false, and it plunged the United States into war. But, you see, when I hear such things, I am dazed and confused. I cannot believe it."

"You cannot believe it? Really? Could you be even more gullible than I thought?"

"Perhaps! However, among the values which were bequeathed to me by our parents, and which are still dear to me, there is trust! How can we live peacefully without trusting our institutions? And all the things you are telling me give me the feeling of being at the heart of a nest of vipers where lies rule."

"I am sorry to disappoint you, my dear, but it is exactly like that. And if you had the opportunity of asking the great authors, they would tell you that there is no government possible without some 'truth adjustment.' Let us take again the example of the Vietnam War. You saw this program. Did you have the impression at any moment that any form of regret was expressed?"

"No."

"Well, this 'mistake,' which was in fact a pretext, cost the lives of how many soldiers and civilians? By using terrorism as a pretext, many actions seem to be justified, Anne, and as disinformation is powerful, not to seek the truth today is a serious matter. Of course, one may doubt all the news or just some of it. One can also protect oneself by pretending that all this is paranoia. But, on the contrary, one can also investigate tirelessly in order to discover and manifest the truth. Think about it for a moment! If we only consider—though the term *only* is itself terrible—the lies related to the September 11 disaster that are well documented and cannot be denied, how can we fail to consider the real danger of the world order, where eugenics plays an important role? How can we refuse to see the reality of these families and of their goal of destruction? How can we ignore these unknown superiors, who make us dance as if we were puppets? How can we turn our eyes away from the staggering show of their manipulations? It is our duty as citizens, Anne, as citizens of the world!"

"It's frightening!"

"You're right; it is frightening. And that is why each human being should feel empowered by this mission of being vigilant."

"We thus have to live in fear!"

"Fear does not move the danger away, Anne. It must be faced, and we need to accept the lessons it teaches us. But, above all, we have to act. When you reread Huxley's *Brave New World*, you will see. That book is relevant for our times."

"I don't even know if I still have it on my bookshelf. I am exhausted, my dear brother."

"I shall offer it to you when we get back, if you like."

"When I am back home, I shall be so tired from all these emotions. I believe I would probably enjoy a book of the Countess of Ségur, like 'A Good Little Devil.'"

John burst out in a loud laugh. "My dear, either you are gifted with a sixth sense or you have already reached a level of extreme fatigue. For today, I shall let you rest, and I shall do the same as well."

John stretched in his seat. Anne had already closed her eyes. Neither one had noticed the two men nearby—always the same except for their attire. Today one was wearing a suit, the other a rather worn-out denim jacket and cowboy boots. One was sleeping, whereas the other was reading the *Times*.

*

Upon arriving in Atlanta, John and Anne rented a car. Anne wanted a Volkswagen. The renter was surprised and said that he did not have any. They took a mid-size Ford and in two hours reached Elberton. After the discrete luxury of the Rappensberger, they were somehow surprised by the style of the Econo Lodge. The building was clean and looked more like a motel. They had not thought to call the hotel to reserve a second room, but luckily there were still rooms available. Their rooms were not adjacent to each other, but that was unimportant. Having other things on their minds, they gave it no further thought, and after unpacking their luggage and taking some rest, they met for dinner. Anne had changed and was wearing a very feminine gray wool dress.

"How elegant! I am delighted to be the one to appreciate it."

"I am tired of always wearing trousers."

"Well, I, as one who advocates skirts and dresses, declare that I am very happy to be seen in your company. In the hotel, they must feel guilty not to have given us two rooms closer to each other."

"You forget that they are holding our passports and that my maiden name is the same as yours; we cannot hide that we're brother and sister."

"Hey, that's right. I hadn't thought about that. What shall we eat?"

"Once again I don't have much appetite. What is the food like in the state of Georgia?"

"I fear that we will be forced to have steak with french fries or red beans."

"Red beans are in Mexico, John!"

"No, no, no! The whole state is contaminated for sure."

"Look at the menu before moaning! Here, you see, they even offer crayfish."

"Lobster yes, crayfish no!"

"I thought that they were very similar?"

"You need to be a purist, I confess, to be able to see the difference, but it is essential and can permanently damage a delicate palate such as mine. I shall thus order one of their steaks; and if it is not tender, there will be trouble!" John was obviously trying to make the atmosphere more relaxed, a little too much in a way.

"I am delighted that you are trying to be funny, but after all the horrible things you made me think about on the airplane, you will admit that you aren't making things easy for me."

"Yes, I know. But we are here now, and we are together. That is the main thing. Tomorrow, then, since your appointment is not until two o'clock, we shall have an excursion in the morning. We shall see the place, and I will give you a few explanations so you will look less naive in front of your unknown superior. I cannot get used to that title. It is annoying not to even know the name of the person one is talking to. You have now reached a point where you should ask his name, it seems to me."

"I shall do better. I want to have a number where I can call him in case I need to. I don't believe he is planning to do me any harm, but if, as you say, he is not working alone, I want to be able to reach him if I feel in danger."

"I am curious to know how he will reply."

"I shall be able to force him. He needs me, and then there is the money he gave me. We are tied to each other until the end of my work, which I have hardly started."

"Don't delude yourself too much. For those people, a few zeros more or less don't make any difference. By the way, you still did not inform Hans that it was such a big amount?"

"No, there will be time for that when all of this is finished."

"You may be right."

They left the restaurant and returned to the hotel. Anne took the elevator while John took the stairs, but neither of them noticed the two men hanging around in the lobby, their faces deep in a tourist flyer. They went out in the park to smoke a cigarette.

*

Even though the rooms were comfortable enough, Anne slept restlessly. She dreamed of stunts in a car; of Nicolas, who cried because he had lost one of his shoes; and of her husband, who was getting angry with her without her knowing why. She woke up in a gloomy mood, feeling a vague anxiety in her stomach. John, on the other hand, exhibited his good mood, albeit artificially. He took all that the breakfast buffet could offer: cereal, toast, bagels, muffins and donuts as well as small pieces of bread. Anne could barely swallow two pieces of toast and a cup of tea.

"What's going on? You didn't sleep well?"

"I had such a terrible night, with strange dreams. They were not dramatic but very destabilizing. Hans and Nicolas were in them. To make a long story short, I am not in great shape."

"That is why a pleasant drive will be a good thing."

"Let's put it this way. It is always dangerous to see things in a negative way, which is how we invite problems."

"Yes, I know. That is what people say."

"I have personally verified the truth of this saying. So chin up. Shall we go, little sister?" With that, they set out and covered the nine miles without additional comment.

A gray sedan was quietly following them at a good distance. The driver knew their destination.

They passed by green pastures, and then the road climbed up until they reached a portion of a knoll where the famous stones of polished granite were standing. Anne remained silent for a while. So *this* was the whole purpose of their journey. The place was solemn, and, even though John had made a brief description, she was impressed by the imposing size of the monument. Anne was facing five massive slabs 20 feet high displayed in the shape of a star. She went around the monument, and then she looked all around to admire the surrounding countryside. She could not help but think of Stonehenge in England or of the ominous monolith in Stanley Kubrick's "2001: A Space Odyssey." On each face of the giant megaliths, the designers had engraved ten commandments in different languages. She came closer, trying to identify these languages and understand the meaning.

John interrupted her reading. "Are you going to fall for that?"

"I would like to understand—to know who erected this monument and why."

"The question is without an answer, my dear. No one knows. And as for why, it is not difficult to understand. The focus is always the same—the world order. Whatever name you use is not important. World order or age of reason—it does not make the slightest difference. What you ought to know is that the monument was erected in 1980, and has been christened the Georgia Guidestones. It is obviously waiting for the end of the world so that its raison d'être can be manifested. Indeed, after the announced apocalypse, the survivors would need such a guide in order to rebuild a new world. The main thing is not so much to rebuild but to bring about an in-depth transformation for a better, purified world. A new civilization, and thus a new order. Do you understand?"

"Yes, of course. It is not difficult to understand. It is less easy to accept these commandments. This requires some analysis, don't you think?"

"You are not the only one of this opinion, and apparently not everyone is comfortable with these ideas. The stones have often been defaced. Some people approve, others don't. Opponents have called them the Ten Commandments of the Antichrist."

"What is the conclusion, then?"

"There is none. Let's wait for the apocalypse. Look, come and see this plaque on the ground. It is supposed to explain a series of intricate notches and holes that correspond to the movements of the sun and stars. The stones would thus serve as a calendar, a clock, and a compass."

Anne read something engraved which said, "Let these be guidestones to an age of reason."

"What a mystery! I would like to know who is behind all this. Is it just one man or a group or an association?"

"The only thing that we know is that one day in June 1979 a certain Robert C. Christian paid a visit to the Elberton Granite Finishing Company. He met the president, Joe Fendley, and asked him for stones, which he wanted hewed, finished, and capable of resisting the most catastrophic events, wherever they may come from. Fendley thought he was a lunatic. However, R. C. Christian strongly insisted. Furthermore, he wanted to be put in contact with a local bank, and that was done. The banker received him with caution, but the man was so elegant and spoke with such distinction that the banker was reluctant to send him off. He listened to him attentively, and finally, though some people were quite reluctant, a deal was concluded with the financial guarantee of a deposit of ten thousand dollars. Obviously, money was not an obstacle, and Fendley was fond of professional challenges. Jackhammers were used to gouge 114 feet into the rock at Pyramid Quarry, searching for hunks of granite big enough to yield the final stones. The first twenty-eight-ton slab was lifted to the surface. I shall not go into the details of the technical problems that had to be faced before they could erect the monument. As you may have guessed, the name R. C. Christian was an alias. Only the banker had to know the man's true identity. The man made the banker promise, though, that his true name would remain secret forever. As far as I know, the secret was perfectly kept. The field was bought at far above its real price, and a lifetime guarantee was made to the owners that they could preserve their pasture. And we are here today, facing this controversial monument, which raises many questions."

"In principle, not everything is bad in these commandments."

"Yes, that's true; for instance, as far as the respect of nature is concerned, you will admit that these are rules of conduct that you and I are observing in our daily life. But beyond that, certain topics, such as reducing the world population, have a vile stench to them."

They started walking back to their car. Anne was not at ease. Her meeting with the unknown superior was making her very nervous. What would he teach her that she did not already know? Would she have to mention the stones in the book? What was their connection with the story of the unknown superior's life? So many things had yet to be clarified, but she had only one desire: to start the work she had been asked to complete, finish it off, and forever close this door, which had opened to a universe that was not hers.

*

After a light lunch of salad and beer, Anne and John returned to the hotel. Though Anne still had fifteen minutes before she went to meet the unknown superior, she found him, dressed in raw silk, already waiting for her in the hall.

"My dear Anne, how are you doing?"

"Well...I'm fine."

"Mmm, really? You're not being totally honest. Am I mistaken?"

"I did not sleep well. In fact, I am not used to being away from home so often, and this is even worse for my son, not to mention my husband."

"Yes, professional obligations may lead us to all kinds of compromise. Having said this, I am sure that the amount on the account at Goldstein's will be able to comfort him."

"I lied to my husband and told him I received forty thousand francs. He would never have accepted the full amount and would have ordered me to give it back. For the first time ever, I had to lie to him, and I am ashamed of it."

"Why did you lie, my dear? Why would one be ashamed to earn money honestly? To this point have I pushed you to do something reprehensible?"

"No, I didn't say that, but you have to know that neither of us places undue importance in money. Our relationship and our child are above all that."

"In this case, why did you accept my proposal and sign at the bank? No one forced you, as far as I know."

"I am still wondering about that, I must confess. But don't worry, I will keep my word and, therefore, complete my mission."

"I know that. People of my age are not mistaken about others." He smiled at her and changed the subject. "I rejoice to make this very small trip with you. I am driving you to see a monument that the oligarchic families have financed, and if you are willing, we shall spend this time in a good-humored atmosphere!" He invited her to take a seat, motioning toward the door the Asian driver was holding open. The driver was the same man who had taken her by boat in Venice.

She had not been talking with John in the morning, and yet the same itinerary seemed to her twice as long. When they arrived at the knoll, the area was still deserted. She saw the driver say a few words to the unknown superior for a few moments, but she did not see the wrinkle on his forehead, showing that he was upset. He approached her and took her by the shoulders in a friendly manner.

"First, I would like to draw your attention once again to numerology. I mentioned the number four, do you remember?"

"I vaguely do."

"The number four symbolizes the action of leaving evil to return to good, and today is October 4. October is the tenth month, isn't it?"

"Yes, yes."

"Well, you should know that the number ten is the symbol of union. I want to believe that we are one, you and I, in this mission to realize the only good thing I shall have ever done in my life." Anne was struck by the tone with which the old man had pronounced this last sentence. Without answering, she looked at him more attentively. He continued. "Observe these stones, read what is engraved there, and give me your opinion."

This time Anne read attentively. In the morning she had noticed the various languages used: English, Russian, Hebrew, Arabic, Hindi, Chinese, Spanish, and Swahili. John had told her that, strangely enough, the United Nations had offered their services for the translation of these commandments. Now she went through the commandments one by one.

The first was to maintain humanity at under 500,000,000 in perpetual balance with nature.

The second was to guide reproduction wisely, improving fitness and diversity.

The third was to unite humanity with a living new language.

The fourth was to rule passion, faith, tradition, and all things with tempered reason.

The fifth was to protect people and nations with fair laws and just courts.

The sixth was to let all nations rule internally, resolving external disputes in a world court.

The seventh was to avoid petty laws and useless officials.

The eighth was to balance personal rights with social duties.

The ninth was to prize truth, beauty, and love, seeking harmony with the infinite.

The tenth was to not be a cancer on the earth but to leave room for nature.

After reading, Anne kept silent.

"So then? What is your impression?"

She took time to answer, and without being aware of it, her tone had something lightly sarcastic. "Tell me, this monument, in a place as wild as Mount Sinai, is it a new version of the tablets of the law of Moses for a new religion?"

He seemed to repress a desire to laugh and watched her attentively. "Clarify your thoughts, Anne. How do you feel about these ten commandments? What do you think about when you read them?"

"The first, the second, and the tenth commandments remind me of the Gaia theory, which believes the earth, including the biosphere, is a physiological dynamic system that has maintained our planet for over three billion years in harmony with life. If one were to take this theory for the truth, the totality of the living beings on the earth would be perceived as a huge organism called Gaia. Gaia would be able to achieve the self-regulation of its components in order to foster life. Mother Earth, like any living organism, would be able to eliminate undesirable enemies like microbes."

"Yes...and then?"

"And then what? What are the microbes? What determines what the 'surplus' is? Perhaps there are five hundred million superior beings and six billion human beings who don't belong here? What criteria are used to decide who is superior and who is inferior? What credentials does one need to have in order to be part of the best? The others will be condemned without further ado, wiped out through incurable sicknesses and other climatic phenomena of great scale that you will not fail to cause! And you dare ask me what I think about it? We see that in movies, you know. It is an excellent plot worth developing for Hollywood, which seems to have been lacking interesting topics in recent years. But those are just movies, right? It is what children are told when they are afraid. And to top it off, we shall have no more traditions or faith, just an eco-religion without God. And you say that you know me well? I am wondering exactly what you expect from me."

"Anne, please calm down. And yet allow an old man, which I am, to tell you that you are very beautiful when you are angry."

"We are not meeting for that purpose, unless I am mistaken."

"Please, let us not fly off the handle. You are right; that is not the purpose. I only wish to make the atmosphere more relaxed, but it seems that I failed."

"Please forgive me. I could imagine the hungry masses of Ethiopia, the people drowning in Haiti, the slaughters in Iraq…"

"I know. I know. I want you to know something, however. Even if all the oligarchic families, including mine, have always been in favor of eugenics, I personally have another philosophy, and I should confess that I embraced it lately. That makes the writing of this book more important, do you understand?"

"Yes, of course, I understand."

"You have to know that those who embrace the theories of eugenics are of all kinds. Take my family, which is famous for the perfection of horse breeding as well as for the high quality of its superior vineyards. I mentioned our marriages, which are decided with great caution, always with the goal of procreating perfect beings and to protect our legacy, of course."

"Horses, vineyards—those are completely acceptable, but we are talking about human beings! And what about consanguinity? You have only to study history! Humanity, as you see it, will degenerate."

"We know that very well too, and our families are, of course, quite careful."

There was a silence. Anne was going around the stones, and she could not calm herself down. "As I hear you speaking, I cannot keep from thinking that all these theories are perfectly fascist, and I am wondering how you expect to impose them on the world. This world is changing, you know; people are no longer so gullible. Having learned from past experiences, they will unite to defend themselves."

"Anne, before blaming, one needs to know. What I am telling you right now does not necessarily match my current philosophy, but this material will be necessary for the writing of the book." The old man stopped talking, apparently exhausted. He had been talking to her for an hour, standing up, leaning on his cane. He made a sign to his driver, who came and unfolded two cloth lawn chairs he had taken out of the trunk. He came back again with a small portable fridge and served them glasses of iced tea.

"Ah! I was sure that you would be thirsty, and now it will be more comfortable to have a chat, don't you think?" At Anne's nod, he continued. "In order to substantiate my sayings, I give you the original version of the protocols that were written more than 150 years ago. You will see the proof of the families' long-time determination to control the world. I suggest that you go through it, even if you don't read the whole document."

Anne flipped through the document, which was about fifty pages. It mostly consisted of a long list of recommendations or actions to be taken. She glanced quickly over a few pages, reading various sections.

The oligarchic power is invincible because it is invisible! By whom or by what will this power be overthrown?

The families are holding in their hands the greatest of all the powers: gold. The sheer bestial stupidity of the dominated and their leaders becomes obvious when we see that they did not think the world would condemn them one day for taking out loans with the burden of paying interest when it would have been simple for them to raise this money from the taxpayers. Instead, they are becoming dependent on the sums they borrow, while the interest rate is increasing every year. Meanwhile, the families were talented enough to present the matter of loans under such a light that world leaders saw only advantages in it. Here is the proof, if need be, of the superiority of the oligarchic mind.

These same dominated people were persuaded that progress would lead them to the reign of reason. What is to be done from now is to undermine faith, to root out any idea of God, to expurgate the soul, and to replace all this with mathematical formula, greed, and material interest. Dominated thinkers are of no use; what we need are workers, downright materialists, and greedy consumers for earthly goods.

The press will be muzzled, even more than today. The enmity among the various social classes will increase when the economic crisis erupts; it will stop financial transactions and all industrial activity. As a result of this event, simultaneously and in all the countries of the world, huge crowds will take to the streets. With demonic joy they will rush to spill the blood of those they have envied since childhood. When this coup d'état is over, it will be possible to tell people, "Everything was going very wrong for you. You are all fed up with so much suffering. We have the power to suppress the cause of your torments—nationalities, borders, the various currencies, and so on. It is thus preferable for the well-being of each country that the power be concentrated in the hands of only one responsible person. This world monarch, elected by our God, will have been initiated in the mysteries.

Anne stopped reading, disgusted by the feeling of superiority that emanated from the authors of the plan, probably important people in finance, whose goal was to establish a totalitarian society ruled by tyrants.

The old man explained, "This document served as a foundation to gain the support of wealthy people for our cause. Even if the text was periodically revised, nothing has been fundamentally changed in 150 years. With the exception of two leaks, it remained hidden from the general public until now. In 1865, Maurice Joly, having been informed about a very first version of the document, used it to write one of his books. He actually plagiarized other authors of his era before committing suicide. And then, there was a second leak in 1903. The plan was published in Russia in a modified version aimed at proving that Jews were trying to rule the world."

"Jews? What on earth do they have to do with this?"

"My dear, among the oligarchic families, many have a Jewish background—like mine for instance—but not all of them. Having said this, when you have to go forward with a plan, the background of the pawns placed on the chessboard does not matter. When you have thoroughly studied the present document, you will better understand the plan conceived for the new order and the world social system. What we actually have is a dynamic, two-step process. First of all, there will be a general destabilization and an increase of free trade. This first step will climax in a social cataclysm. During the second step, a new hierarchy of society will be established. A smart person like you will be able to realize that we are at the dawn of launching this second step. We will witness an unprecedented world social crisis. We are only at the dawn of the financial crisis, which will turn into an economic crisis. It is very possible to ruin and starve entire nations by using the futures exchange, and the families have been able to convince the world that food is a financial instrument that can be used to speculate. Originally, this market simply guaranteed producers and buyers a price on future production or breeding, but now the immense majority of the exchanges on this market are made with fictive, non-existent food."

"That is not possible," Anne said, nervously holding her glass of tea. She seemed to be astounded.

"It is perfectly possible! You just need to have enough money to manipulate the price up or down. The concept was tested in 2006. It was important to know if it would work on a larger scale when the time comes. At the end of 2006, there was a sharp rise in the price of food products worldwide. In one year, the price of wheat increased 80 percent, the price of corn 90 percent, and the price of rice 320 percent. Two hundred million people, mostly children, no longer had access to food and there were riots in thirty countries. Then, in 2008, the prices mysteriously fell; the true final offensive will take place later. If it is not enough to create financial and economic chaos and to starve populations, the families will launch a third world war by pitting religions against one another. And ultimately, according to the plan described in the old document, the situation will be favorable and a credulous humanity will cry out in gratitude for the tyrants who will offer them this new world. They will not realize that the new system will simply be used to dominate them even more."

Anne felt fire in her cheeks, and exploded. "I can't believe you! This is a diabolical plan and it won't work. Look at what happened with the society established by Stalin; in many ways, you have the same ideas. The people were in extreme poverty in 1917. Lenin, Stalin, and others, managed to build a world that looked better, but they did so by muzzling the populations. One day, however, they woke up and saw the result. Another point is when your old document refers to a sovereign elected by God, aren't you exaggerating? We are in the twenty-first century; people are informed and gullibility has started declining with the emergence of the Internet. People can read between the lines, you know."

"The families are aware of all that. It is one of their top concerns, and everything is now in place in terms of disinformation. What I mean is that you can find diametrically opposed points of view on the Internet. Don't say that you never realized that; I would not believe you."

"Groups of uncorrupted and courageous people will appear to fight the families!"

"We have anticipated that. These movements will be infiltrated by agents trained in intelligent and active disinformation. In any case, both camps have always been infiltrated simultaneously; it is an efficient technique that has been tested successfully. The families even created movements of opposition that could be controlled. The big families are financing the revolutions, Anne! First of all, we financed the communist revolution. The churches themselves were infiltrated; the wealth of the oligarchs is so huge that anything is possible. There is indeed a risk, but it is so small! You would need completely independent individuals, who would keep themselves informed and would encourage other individuals to do the same. They would then be able to spread the truth to the world, even on a small scale. You would need people who reflect and build up a real critical mind, people who listen to their inner conscience. This will help you grasp the importance of your mission, Anne. Today the media, with no reluctance, is doing their work of stupefying the masses by delivering messages focused exclusively on entertainment or on hidden messages. I hope from the bottom of my heart that the book you are going to write will trigger a quest for the truth, the absolute truth. Only one person, to my knowledge, really understood the danger of what was behind the document of 1903, and that person was Aleksandr Solzhenitsyn. The proof of this is that, frightened by what he had discovered, he prohibited the publication of his study before his death. This sentence remains: 'The design of this plan is far above the capacities of an ordinary soul, including that of its author.'"

"I am trying to understand what motivates these families, all these people who can acquire anything, these people who have never experienced want, who have never worried what tomorrow may bring, who have never felt the anxiety of no longer having employment and thus losing the capacity to honor one's commitments. I wonder how they can live with themselves. What are these oligarchs thinking about when they wake up in the morning? What motivates them, makes them smile, and pours joy into their hearts? Perhaps they are left only with the perverse satisfaction of destroying and crushing others, these others before whom they never carry out self-examination , that is for sure. You want me to say what I think of all that? I pity them. I pity you. I wondered—and am still wondering—why do you want me to write this book? You did not give me a complete answer. I shall write the book because I committed myself to doing it, and it will be widely distributed so that it will have the importance you want it to have, but it may not be enough to secure your redemption, I fear. Forgive me if I seem too severe."

"I accept your severity, Anne, and I understand it. But my briefing is not over yet. It is already four o'clock. Aren't you tired?"

"I am tired, but I am listening to you."

"All right. I talked much about finance. I shall now touch upon another aspect of what we may call the system of the families. There are twelve families altogether, as I think I already told you. Under these families, there are hundreds of very rich individuals who collaborate more or less directly in the objective of advancing their plans. Over the centuries, common financial interests have brought these twelve families together out of a desire to concentrate more and more power in their hands and also out of a deep feeling of superiority. Progressively, an ideological convergence was established on the foundation of a common spiritual belief. I shall not be able to go into too much historical detail; it would be too long and perhaps not very useful. But you need to understand the current situation."

"Go ahead. I am listening to you."

"I shall begin by talking about the Kabbalah, which is a very old, esoteric tradition of Judaism that had an occult-like influence for many centuries. This tradition came to include numerous trends throughout history. A particular trend is the one that developed when the Jews were held as captives in Babylon for seventy years. This trend turned itself toward the occult and magical forces and was strongly influenced by a pagan cult. This cult emanated from a very old mythology, which was grounded in the fertility cult and connected to the cycle of seasons. Every winter, the 'God who dies' went down to the inferior world, where he reigned over the dead and the demons. And then every year, this God resurrected with the return of the beautiful season. This God who dies was an evil God, a usurper, who had defeated the creator God, who was a good God. Thus, the God who dies reigned, and he was to be appeased by sacrifice. It was the worst kind of sacrifice—that of children. The ritual had to imitate the resurrection of the god, so the participants took a hallucinogenic drug that they thought would give them access to an invisible reality, help them develop paranormal powers, and enable them to be possessed by demons. In this state, they would kill young children, eat their flesh, and drink their blood so that the dead God could be reborn in them and give them great powers. These ceremonies also included sexual orgies as well as holy marriages between male and female priests in order to give birth to sons of God."

"Forgive me, but even though we are outside, I feel as if I need air. I shall walk a little bit, if you please."

"Of course. I understand."

Anne walked a few feet away and made a considerable effort not to shout or simply run away. Did she really have to listen to all these awful revelations? What else would she discover? What kind of crazy religion did these rich families expect to establish in their new world? She had a painful thought for Nicolas, who, again this evening, would go to bed without his mother. She breathed deeply and sat down again.

"I understand that my story is overwhelming, Anne, but it is necessary. The influence of the Kabbalah continued for centuries; it can be traced in the texts of Plato and then during the twelfth century in the Templars and then again during the seventeenth century in Rosicrucianism. This sect of alchemists was obsessed by the quest of the philosopher's stone, which would be able to turn lead into gold. Finally, the Kabbalah infiltrated freemasonry. However, despite this common foundation, one should not imagine that all the families share the same religious convictions. There are different interpretations, starting from a common central theme. But let us put this topic aside for the moment. I see that time is passing, and I fear that you might be cold since the weather is chilly. I shall bring you back to your hotel so that you may rest, and I suggest that we resume this conversation tomorrow morning, what do you think about that?"

"Yes, I think that is a good idea."

"Would nine o'clock be a good time for you?"

"Yes."

"By the way, is the hotel comfortable enough?"

"Yes, it is quite good."

"I am sorry that I could not find a more pleasant place for you, but Elberton has very few hotels and both are about the same level."

"Don't worry about that. I have everything I need."

*

John was relieved when Anne appeared at his door, though he could not help but notice her weariness "Ah, here you are! You look so pale."

"I am exhausted. He has spoken throughout the afternoon, and my brain is boiling. I am going to take a bath, and I shall give you a brief report during dinner. Would that be all right?"

"Yes, I can see that you are burned out. By the way, I sent a message to Hans to tell him that everything was going well."

"Well, that was a good idea because I feel unable to do that myself."

"You see—one always needs an elder brother nearby."

"Oh, John, I almost forgot. Please have a look at this before dinner," Anne said, handing her brother the manuscript. "The unknown superior told me that these are the protocols explaining how to establish their new world. It is edifying, as you will see. A sort of North Korea on a world scale."

After Anne left, John closed the door of his room with a heavy heart. What on earth had this man talked about for over three hours, and why was she in such a state? He knew the strength of his sister's character, but he was more and more worried. He sat in an armchair and started to read the protocols.

*

Shin Jon Gol was fuming. What kind of boring mission had been given to him! Was there a lack of novices in the organization? The capacities of a beginner would have been sufficient for this job. And with all that, he had to deal with a non-existent colleague he was obliged to drag along.

The trip had been uninteresting, the hotel was of the worst possible kind, and now this old dinosaur had no better idea than to organize his meeting with the woman in front of those stones, out in the middle of nowhere. It had been impossible, in such a place, to properly intercept their conversation, despite the extremely modern listening device he was using.

What he would send to Karl was terrible, and once more that disagreeable guy would criticize and humiliate him. He had set up the crappy mikes everywhere, but that hadn't been enough. The main discussion had taken place up there, on the knoll. And he knew what Karl would say: he had done a bad job; he should have used more sophisticated devices. But who would have thought that the old guy would choose such a place? Or did the old man suspect something? He would have to be careful from now on, and Karl had to be informed. There was, however, some news he could bring to his attention. The lady was not alone. First, he had thought that it was her lover because the guy did not look like her husband. But he was kissing her on the cheeks and they were not sharing a room. It was when he listened to their conversation at the breakfast table that he had heard him call her "little sister." So, then, she had a protector. Karl would be delighted to learn that.

*

The old man did indeed suspect something, and his driver had spotted their shadow. Karl had thus devised some plan for tailing Anne. He was suspicious, as could be expected. Bob phoned Karl.

"Hello, dear friend. What is the latest news?"

"There are only good things to report, my friend, only good things."

"That is true; I have seen that you have established surveillance around the young woman."

"Yes, I wouldn't want anything bad happening to you."

"I knew I could count on you, and by the way, though I trust her completely, you will be kind enough to forward the surveillance reports to me."

"Of course, of course."

"As long as I am with her, nothing bad will take place. She is charming and meek, as you must have been told."

"You were the very first to say that, dear friend, but one never knows. Among spiritual brethren, we always have to be careful. Our great master is very concerned about us, all of us."

"Yes, of course. Well, you can then see that I am making giant steps. Anne is intelligent; I had already understood that. But she is now captivated by the topic, and I am more and more convinced that she will write a book of great quality. I have almost finished with her education. She will be ready for the thirty-first."

"I have no doubt about that, and I wish you much success."

"Thank you again, dear friend."

"You are welcome!"

The old man was exhausted. He rested his head on the headrest and said with a tired voice, "Young, we go back."

The driver began driving.

*

John and Anne met again for dinner, and John asked whether she had been able to get some rest.

"A little, but not enough. Did you have some time to go through the document?"

"Yes, it is frightening, but it didn't tell me anything I didn't already know. This just confirms the inscriptions on the stones and what I told you this morning."

"The unknown superior gave me additional explanations on their strategy, from the fictitious price increase of food products in order to create starvation to the economic situation, which is just starting to collapse. This is frightening, John. What will happen to us?"

"Listen, don't let this get to you. It will not take place. There are enough people who are attentive and vigilant. This handful of individuals doesn't carry that much weight."

"That's what I told him, but he explained their strategy. If the attentive and vigilant people you are talking about gather in associations, they infiltrate these associations and..."

"Anne, come back to earth! This guy is destroying you. Listen to him with one ear and write his book, but that's all. Life, our life, is different. You have a husband whom you love and a lovely son. Don't let this crush you, please."

"Yes, you're right; I'm becoming as gullible as a girl of sixteen. Excuse me. I'll be back in a minute. I need to talk to Hans."

Hans answered as if he already had his hand on the telephone, even though it was two o'clock in the morning in Basel.

"My darling, it is you, at last!"

"Yes, my love. It's good to hear your voice! Did I wake you?"

"Never mind. So what is going on?"

"For the moment, nothing special. John took me to see the stones this morning, and he gave me some explanations."

"I know; he sent me an e-mail."

"And the unknown superior came to pick me up at two o'clock. He talked to me all afternoon about the world of finance and of those who are pulling the strings; it was interesting but tiring. I am exhausted. We will finish tomorrow morning. I hope to get a flight quickly and to be back with you two. How is Nicolas?"

"I do my best to entertain him, but he misses you. He would like you to be here to give him a big hug."

"Oh! Don't tell me that."

"You would like things to be otherwise?"

"No, of course not, but it makes me feel bad."

"Take care of yourself, darling. Don't be manipulated."

"No, don't worry. And John is here."

"That's good. I love you!"

"Me too. Many kisses."

Upon putting down the receiver, Anne again held back an irrepressible desire to cry, telling herself that it was not the time to break down. She powdered her face and went back to the table.

They ate their dinner half-heartedly and made an appointment to meet the next morning at eight o'clock for breakfast. It was out of the question to take risks and let the unknown superior arrive before nine and notice the presence of John.

*

The next day, the bright sunshine invaded the room and Anne realized that she had not even thought to close the curtains. This beautiful light was a good sign. One more morning session and she would be able to think about the trip back without worrying. Even if later she had to travel elsewhere, she could again immerse herself in the happy atmosphere of her life as a spouse and mother until then. For the moment, nothing else mattered. She chose a blue outfit which suited her well and went down to meet John. He was already waiting for her in the dining room.

"Ah! This time, I see that you slept well."
"I took a sleeping pill."
"Why?"
"To sleep well, obviously. I really needed it."
"Well, it is true that, in some cases, these drugs can be a good relief; the main point is not to use them too much."
"You know me."
"That's why I don't make a big fuss!"

This time, they had a quick breakfast. By 8:30, John was back in his room and Anne was waiting in the hall. The car of the unknown superior arrived and parked—fifteen minutes early again. Anne wondered whether he was trying to take her by surprise. By not telling him about the presence of John, she had told him a lie, and she did not feel comfortable about that. The driver was already opening the door as she approached the car.

"My dear, Anne, did you sleep well? Did you have a good rest?"
"Yes, thank you, but I won't hide the fact that I owe my good sleep to the use of a sleeping pill."
"Too bad, indeed, but I understand. Yesterday was a little heavy, wasn't it?"
"I wouldn't say that, but I was exhausted, I have to admit."
"Today, I shall take less time, and I think you will be able to prepare for your trip back."

"That's good. My son needs me."

"I understand, and that is why I thought it was a good thing to come a little earlier."

"You were staying nearby?"

"Well, many places in the world can serve as a pied-à-terre."

Anne did not insist. She saw that the car was heading again to the knoll and could not help but ask, "Are we going back to see the stones one more time?"

"Yes. The place is particularly fit for the revelations I have to tell you. Furthermore, it is calm and discreet and I like that. But don't worry, we have the chairs we used yesterday and hot coffee. My driver has even thought of white blankets in case the morning is chilly. Yesterday I regretted not having them with us."

"But the sun is shining."

"Yes. That is even better."

When they reached the monument, they sat down, as they had the day before, not far from the stones, and the driver immediately served coffee and biscuits.

"First of all, Anne, I wanted to say that I am happier and happier with our collaboration. I feel that we understand each other and that we are establishing a good connection, and this gives me a warm feeling."

"All the things you are teaching me are quite troubling, but you don't seem like someone belonging to the circle of people you are describing."

"I shall tell you more about that, Anne, but not today. We finished yesterday speaking about the system of families, didn't we?"

"Yes."

"Today I would like to talk to you about my family in particular, and I shall start with the Khazars. Do you know anything about them?"

"I know almost nothing."

"Well, the Khazars were Turkish semi nomads in central Asia. At the end of the eighth century or the beginning of the ninth century, the Khazar elite, and perhaps a part of the population, converted to Judaism. That is how the Jews of Eastern Europe are more or less descendants of the Khazars, who migrated westward between the tenth and the twelfth centuries when the Khazar Empire collapsed. Actually, the black nobility of Venice, which I already mentioned, has a mostly Khazar background. My family, Anne, can be traced back to the Khazars. In 1648, my ancestors followed the cabalist preacher Sabbatai Zevi, who claimed to be the messiah who would bring together the Jewish tribes. Many communities recognized him with an incredible enthusiasm as the Messiah of the Jews, destined to bring the Jewish people back to the holy land and to re-establish the kingdom of Israel. Many of them were preparing to go and started selling their belongings. In the beginning of 1666, Sabbatai headed for Constantinople now called Istanbul, the capital of the Ottoman Empire. Nathan of Gaza, his prophet, had announced that he would place the Sultan's crown on Sabbatai's head. Unfortunately for Sabbatai, he was denounced as a troublemaker to the Ottoman authorities by the leaders of the local Jewish community. Sabbatai was put in jail in Istanbul, and in September 1666, probably fearing for his life, converted to Islam. When this conversion was announced, the disappointment and shock were as strong as the indescribable hope he had raised up. Many waited, thinking this to be a short-term strategy, but progressively, most of his followers abandoned him, including my ancestors. In 1775, Jacob Frank claimed to be the direct successor of Sabbatai Zevi and claimed to have received revelations. According to these revelations, all that had been formally prohibited by the Torah was from that point on allowed in the messianic age."

Anne started with surprise.

"Yes, I know. This may sound incredible to you, but the explanation that the Messiah would come only when humanity was immersed in sin and chaos was accepted. The practices of Frankism included orgiastic and pedophilic rites deemed as heretical by the Jewish authorities of the time. It was probably out of a desire to escape the persecution of the Jews that Frank and his disciples converted to Christianity, but they made it clear that it had to be a visible transition toward a future Messianic religion. And this did not bring an end to the occult practices. This is how my seventh-generation ancestor, a Sabbatean-Frankist banker of Frankfurt with close business connections to the sovereign of the time, Frederick II of Hessen-Kassel, contacted Adam Weishaupt. Have you ever heard of Adam Weishaupt, Anne?"

Anne preferred to lie. "Vaguely. He was connected to freemasonry, wasn't he?"

"Hold on, here is the copy of a letter in German. You read German, don't you?"

"Yes, my husband is a German-speaking Swiss."

"As you can see, it is signed by Brother Spartacus and is dated 1773."

Anne skimmed the document. It was a letter of gratitude. Brother Spartacus was grateful to his brother for putting him in contact with such wealthy people during their last meeting. He said that the financial means available to him would give him the possibility of establishing a pure and illuminated freemasonry, which would be able to create a new world.

"You see, Anne, my ancestor understood that by infiltrating freemasonry, he could lead from behind the scenes and increase his wealth. He was therefore using Weishaupt also called Spartacus. Besides that, the Bavarian Illuminati had a considerable influence on the Masonic lodges. The American presidents Washington and Jefferson, for instance, were fervent defenders of Weishaupt, but I don't want to bore you with too many historical details. Then, in 1830, under the leadership of a certain Albert Pike and other freemasons, one can see the historical outcome of the cult followed by the twelve families. Pike was the first great occultist pope of this religion; he organized and structured it in a rite called Palladism."

"I have never heard of this rite."

"Of course not. The families have taken exceeding care that it remains secret. Only a traitor, Diana Vaughan, a priestess of Palladism who later converted to Catholicism, unveiled some secrets about one hundred years ago."

When the name of this woman was mentioned, Anne showed a particular interest. "What happened to her?"

"Of course, she was threatened by her old Palladist friends, and consequently she was in danger. After her conversion she remained secluded in a monastery, but she wanted to denounce her old beliefs. She then met a publisher named Leo Taxil. A friendship grew between both, and he published some of her confessions, which aroused strong interest. While trying to check the authenticity of these revelations, the press wanted to meet her personally. The Palladists then hatched a diabolical plan—to assassinate her would have added to her credibility, so something else had to be done. In April 1897, Diana Vaughan was to appear in public and give a lecture organized by Leo Taxil. But a few hours before that, the latter delivered her to his Palladist friends. He appeared himself to the press and claimed that he had invented everything. Diana Vaughan was discredited forever. You see, Anne, the families are the champions of disinformation, and no traitor can hope to be seen as credible!"

"Except you, maybe?"

"In the present case, there is no betrayal, Anne, and I have no doubt that you will understand when you are completely informed."

"What were the beliefs of the Palladists, then?"

"In fact, they spring from freemasonry, which is not a homogeneous block but consists of many different lodges. A vast majority of the masons are mostly interested in the advantages that they receive from the organization. In theory they want only what is good for each other, have no bad intentions toward others, and don't understand much about the deep meaning of the rites. Anyway, they become enlightened as they progress in the Masonic hierarchy. The information received brings them closer and closer to Palladism. However, even among those in the highest grades, if an initiate is deemed unfit, he will never have access to the truth proclaimed by the most obscure lodges. It is no coincidence that, during the Enlightenment period, the establishment of the central bank of England in 1694 roughly matched the considerable expansion of freemasonry in England. For the aristocracy of this time, to be a freemason was seen as chic. And one should know that the freemasons have clearly done good things. For instance, they unified the colonies of the United States by proclaiming valuable ideals such as civil liberties and equal opportunities for all. However, even though the freemasons claim to be the sons of light, these ideals were used to gain power and were never really implemented. Moreover, ever since the Enlightenment period, Western civilization has been grounded in the denial of a creator God, even though God gave a goal to human life. Under the influence of the ideals springing from the Enlightenment, the man of the street feels free and sees the government, education, and the media as relatively open and democratic. For him, evil is disorganized and is mainly caused by human weakness. People are gradually initiated to Palladism, which is presented via a certain philosophy and during some ceremonies, like those of the Bohemian Club. I am inviting you to attend such a ceremony."

"You are asking me if I agree to attend this kind of thing? My first thought would be to say no."

"This can be very useful for the writing of the book, Anne. It is a professional act. You see, this philosophy is organized around two poles: one is superficial, and the other is deeper, more spiritual. Let us start with the first one."

"Excuse me. I would like to have a cup of coffee, please."

"Oh, forgive me! I am neglecting my duties."

The driver came to serve them and offered Anne a blanket, which she accepted. The early morning sunshine was now gone, and heavy storm clouds were approaching. Her blue outfit did little to protect her from the wind, which had just started blowing.

After seeing to the refreshments and blanket, the old man continued. "I shall try to be precise and brief. Externally speaking, this philosophy can be summarized as such: the values are to tolerate whatever is opposed to the established order. The key goals are reason, progress, personal interest, knowledge, and materialism. The things to be banned are religion, which is harmful superstition, and universal values. The things to be promoted, in the name of neutrality, are secularism and whatever is relative. God must be hated, the conscience in itself does not exist, and what counts is power. And power gives the illusion to be God. The goal is not what is good but what is useful. The end justifies the means. You have to sacrifice others for the sake of personal interest."

Anne shook her head, as if refusing something obviously wrong. He continued, "I understand what kind of affect this list may have on you, Anne, but it is necessary to understand the whole picture. This philosophy is based on the premise that a new world will emerge only out of total chaos—hence the need to encourage the collapse of family values; empty the places of worship; provoke perpetual change in order to create confusion; eliminate the notion of authority in societies, schools, and families; and trigger cultural revolutions. The goal is to create a society ruled by money and sex. Children must be exposed to sex from their young age; pornography must be promoted. Joy comes from victory, not from peace. Man must free himself from his moral and religious bonds. He should explore his repressed desires, his inner darkest self, because it will give him joy, and joy is a source of strength. Human beings should be in a constant state of revolt because they are never satisfied. They should be thirsty for ever-greater endeavors. The media is given instructions in order to inculcate this change of behavior by all means. The one who shares this vision is then ready to discover the deepest and the most spiritual part, which is Palladism."

  The man paused slightly before going on. "The world is ruled by a reality that is invisible to the physical eyes but truly visible to the spiritual eyes. Everybody has these spiritual eyes but does not use them. The God of the religions really exists but is an oppressor who created men in order to turn them into slaves whose only destiny is to worship and attend to this God. He wants to keep man in ignorance; he is the God of domination. Lucifer is the good God. He rebelled against this oppression and came in order to liberate man by guiding him to the forbidden tree, which symbolizes, according to him, the knowledge of magic and supernatural powers. Lucifer claims to be the prince of light, the one who represents knowledge. Like a sun, he wants to shine on humanity. He comes to liberate man, and this liberation is revealed by exploring the most obscure part of himself. Free from all his fetters, man becomes God himself and recovers the full possession of his abilities and talents.

Lucifer is the true father of humanity. We are his children, the sons of light. His cleverest move was to claim that he does not exist. And, indeed, how can one protect oneself from an enemy who does not exist? But believe me, Lucifer is very real, as are the entities that evolve around him. There are good reasons why religions call him the prince of this world. He grants luck and prosperity to those who worship him. By taking certain drugs, anyone is able to revive his spiritual gifts and see the invisible realities. Anyone who attends this kind of ceremony will have a very strong experience and will suddenly have the impression of possessing supernatural forces of infinite potential, which will, of course, lead this person to believe that Lucifer is good. Traditional religions portray Lucifer as the archangel of evil; according to the new Palladian religion, it is a major injustice. Lucifer represents good and God evil. Lucifer is severe but he is good. Only his enemies have reason to fear him. Regarding the practical aspect, the cult is organized around cells guided by a father and a mother. There are many more followers than you may imagine. I am not talking about these extravagant figures completely dressed in black and covered with tattoos. They are dropouts who have nothing to do with Palladism. The true followers look like normal people, with no special external signs. Are you still following me, Anne?"

She gave the impression of being lost in her own thoughts. "I'm following you. It is not that I am incredulous, but I am increasingly perplexed. If I understand you well, we are facing a complete inversion of values. What is good for me would be bad for a Luciferian and vice versa. There wouldn't be any absolute standard of goodness. In a Luciferian society, no one would accept his position and rank and all that would matter would be to dominate others and spread what I would call evil. Is my understanding correct?"

"That is actually the way they view things, but there are several schools of thought and action, just as in all religions since the dawn of time. But I have to talk to you about those who are still sticking to the old rites, especially the rite of the resurrection of the God who dies. These are people who still practice human sacrifices even today. Young girls are raped, and when they are pregnant, the birth is provoked during a ceremony where starving dogs are unleashed. Those who watch these atrocities either affect a complete indifference by claiming to be infinitely superior and therefore without qualms or, after seeing the babies crucified or impaled, are so shocked that they become completely distorted. In any case, they have made a pact with demons, which will assist them but above all will manipulate them. It may also happen that young girls are forced to attend these ceremonies and the traumas are such that they may develop multiple personalities. They will then be exploited at will, and this is all without any danger for the Luciferian. Whatever testimonies they may want to present, they are so damaged that their stories would have absolutely no credibility. Who would believe such a thing in 2010?"

Anne was speechless. Again, she couldn't breathe well. The sky was dark and seemed to refuse any possibility for the sunbeams to break through. She was very cold.

"My dear Anne, it displeases me greatly to upset you in this way, but I must give you complete information. Otherwise, the book would fail to achieve its goal—my goal, I should say. It will be the most beautiful achievement of my life, the only one probably, and this will be possible only with your help. I am grateful to you, Anne."

She looked at him, alarmed by his last words. "I'm speechless."

"I know. This is beyond the limits of imagination. You should know, however, that the twelve are not the starting point of these abominations. Of course they maintain very strong occult relations with the demons, seeing them as good spiritual entities, but it goes no further than this. Convinced of their superiority, they have kept their objective, throughout the centuries, to maintain a pure lineage in order to preserve the spiritual powers they gain from generation to generation by being intimate with the demons. Don't believe that the leading elite have come from completely independent families! You may or may not know it, but twenty American presidents were freemasons of a high grade, and you can verify that forty-two of them are directly or indirectly descendants of the English king John Plantagenet, a mediocre king famous for being inclined toward lust. To have all the information you need, you must attend a ceremony of the Bohemian Club. I shall give you all the details."

"It is out of question! You never told me that I would have to endure all that!"

"Don't worry. In the Bohemian Club, you will see only re-enactments. Don't be mistaken: I never contemplated even one moment to mistreat you. But I want you to meet the people who attend these meetings. It will be very educational, as you will see."

"Is that all for today?"

"Yes, Anne, I shall let you digest this story. Though it is heavy, I thought that it was necessary. And it had to take place here, in front of these stones, which bear witness to my statements."

Without a word, they went back to the hotel. She got out of the car, gave him her hand, and told him, in a tone that brooked no reply, "I shall not ask your name, I know that you will not give it to me, but I want a telephone number to reach you in case of danger."

"Why are you asking this of me?"

"You told me that you don't want to cause me any harm?"

"Yes, of course."

"So give me your number!" she said, raising her voice.

"But I don't understand."

"You don't understand? I am afraid, that is all! Is that what you wanted to hear? I am afraid even of you but, above all, of the others. From now on, I fear I'll be afraid of my shadow! I have a family waiting for me, in case you have forgotten, and a little boy who needs his mother! Should I understand that, if I were in danger, you would let me down?"

"No, of course not!"

"All right, then give me your number, please!" She was holding out her hand with a peremptory attitude. He took out a piece of paper and wrote a phone number.

"You may reach me any time."

"I hope so! And when is the next excursion?"

"Anne, please don't be upset. I did only what was necessary to validate your work. In relation to you, I promise you, my intentions are pure."

"Yes, excuse me, but this is my way of dealing with the shock. I have nothing against you, really."

"I shall call you within a few days in order to organize your departure to Spain, where you will attend the Bilderberg meeting."

"Ah, Spain this time?"

"I already mentioned it to you, didn't I?"

"I can't remember, but let's go to Spain. See you there!"

"Have a nice trip back! And please enjoy your nice little family."

Anne had already turned her back and entered the lobby of the hotel.

*

This mission was turning into a disaster for Shin Jon Gol. He had instructed his colleague to put microphones in John's and Anne's rooms, and the idiot had not understood correctly. Only Anne's room had been equipped, even though they had met in John's room in Ingolstadt! Shin sent him to complete his task as soon as John had come down for breakfast, but those two idiots had eaten at full speed. Shin had tried to inform his accomplice that Anne was leaving alone and John was coming back to his room, but it was too late. He was now coming down with a crumpled shirt and mussed up hair.

"Look at yourself! Where are you coming from?" Shin demanded.

"From his room, what do you think?"

"What happened?"

"He just laid into me! He's no wimp, I'll tell you that."

"And?"

"What do you think I should do?"

"Where is he now?"

"He is knocked out on the floor."

"And the chambermaid, you imbecile!"

"Hey, come on! I put the Do not Disturb sign on his door."

"Yes, you put the Do not Disturb sign out, but now the chambermaid will be in the corridors, idiot! How are you going to take him out of there—through the keyhole?"

"We'll find a way to distract the chambermaid. If she's cute, I'll touch her up, and while we talk I trust you to do what has to be done."

Shin shrugged his shoulders resignedly. As a matter of fact, professionals were rarely encountered in this line of work. The idiot had at least one good point. To make up for his lack of brains, he had herculean force. When they reached John's room, Shin saw that the blow on the neck had been enough; John's vertebrae were crushed.

"Pack up his things, everything! Put everything in the suitcase, even the bathroom stuff."

"We're taking his luggage too? What for? There is nothing interesting in there."

"The point is not to recover anything but to make believe that he has simply gone without giving a forwarding address, you idiot! Investigations will not start immediately. Where did you learn this line of work? From your grandmother?"

"Hey, enough is enough, OK?"

Shin left John's phone on the desk, and they left the room with the body and the luggage. Fortunately the corridor was deserted. Nothing and no one had witnessed what, for them, was merely a small incident.

When Shin called Karl to inform him, he just said, "You are damned lucky, boys."

*

Anne almost ran to John's room. She knocked at the door and called. There was no answer. She went back to the lobby.

"Excuse me. Did you see my brother go out? He is in room number 209."

"I did not see him, Madam. He is probably in the garden."

"Yes, I shall see."

Anne searched the garden, the swimming pool, and the sports hall before coming back and checking the dining room, the lounge, and the bar. John was nowhere. She checked her phone—no messages. She called him, but there was no answer. Suddenly feeling anxious, she returned to the reception desk.

"Sir, is it possible to enter room 209? I went around the hotel and could not find my brother anywhere. It is all the more abnormal as he was waiting for me. I would like to make sure that he is all right."

"One moment please, Madam. I will inform the manager."

The manager arrived, frowning. "Madam, we don't usually enter rooms where clients are residing."

"I understand, sir, but I have been around the hotel in vain, trying to find my brother. He has not answered my telephone calls, and I have been knocking on the door of his room. He must be in there . I am afraid that he has had an attack of some kind."

"Did you see him this morning?"

"Yes. We had breakfast together, and I left him at eight forty-five. I just came back to the hotel. Please! Don't take the risk of failing to assist a person in danger."

This last point removed the misgivings of the manager, and they headed toward the room.

"He has put the Do not Disturb sign on his door. Perhaps he is sleeping."

"This is not like him. Knock on the door! Knock more loudly! John! Please open! Please!"

The manager used his master key, and they entered. Everything was in order; the bed was unmade, but the sheets were smoothed out. The curtains and the window were open. Anne entered the bathroom and saw the shelves were empty. There was no suitcase; only John's phone was on the desk. She burst into tears.

"Madam, what is obvious is that your brother left without paying!"

"My brother did not leave!"

"And yet it looks like he did. May I know who will pay the bill?"

"Don't bother me about your bill. I shall pay everything. For the moment, I want you to call the police. My brother has disappeared."

"Your brother is an adult. I doubt that the police will want to come here, but if you insist, I will tell you how to get there. First, though, Madam, I must ask you to leave a deposit."

Anne took five one-hundred-dollar bills from her bag. "Will that be enough?"

"Of course! Don't get me wrong, but we see so many strange situations..."

"Spare me your comments and tell me where the nearest police station is!"

They went back to the reception desk. The manager seemed contrite. He unfolded a road map, showed the location of the motel, and indicated the road to the police station.

"Ask for Officer Spencer. He is a friend of mine."

"Thank you."

Anne ran to the parking lot, followed by the employee. She tried in vain to insert the key in the keyhole; her hands were trembling convulsively.

"Madam, let me do this for you. If I may give you some advice, you should not drive in your state. Come and drink something and calm down a bit..."

"I can't. I have to act quickly, and I can't explain why."

"As you like, but please be careful."

"Yes, I shall try."

Anne sat down, clasping her hands, trying to stop this irrepressible shaking without much success. She started in a screech of tires but was forced to stop on the roadside after five hundred yards. She realized that she was in no shape to drive her car. She tilted her seat backward, kept the window wide open, and breathed deeply, knowing that in such circumstances, her worst enemies were panic and anger. She had to avoid these two traps and preserve her powers of analysis and synthesis. She closed her eyes and, with superhuman effort, tried to reflect on the possible solutions.

The first solution that came to her was to call the unknown superior for help. Immediately, though, she realized that such a move was impossible. She would have to inform him of John's presence with her, thus confessing her fear, her lack of confidence in him, and her lying by omission. Moreover, something was telling her that the unknown superior had nothing to do with John's disappearance. The second solution was to seek the help of her husband, Hans, who loved her deeply and had always been a steady source of moral support. But this solution was also impossible. Nicolas needed a quiet and relaxed dad. By informing Hans, Anne would cause him to be worried. And what could he do, in reality?

She wondered who else she could think of. Hans's parents were dead. Her own father was now living in South Africa, and her mother, seriously impaired after a stroke, had been admitted the year before to a specialized institution. There was no help to be expected from that direction. Unfortunately, the only hope remaining was with the police and the benevolence of this Officer Spencer. The disappearance of a man in his forties, in full mental and physical health, would make one want to smile, that was for sure, because a love affair would seem most likely.

Anne had left the car and was taking a few steps. She looked at the sky and visualized Nicolas peacefully falling asleep in his bed around this time. Her duty clearly appeared to her. First, she had to mobilize all her resources. She had to trust life, trust John, and trust the American police. She had to give the police the image of a balanced woman, not of a frantic, crazy girl; she would need to clearly describe the situation. The point, however, was that the source of her anxiety could not be disclosed. The manager of the hotel would be questioned; he would undoubtedly talk about the car of the unknown superior, which had not gone unnoticed, and mention that on the previous day in the afternoon as well as this morning, Anne had left her brother at the hotel to follow this obviously very rich old man. No doubt the police would take this information and would see a connection between the two facts, a connection that she could not clarify. She returned to the car and drove on, her heart feeling deadly cold.

*

The Elberton police station was a drab, boring rectangle, like any police station in the world. Anne talked to an employee, who lifted colourless eyes toward her.

"I am here to report a disappearance, sir. May I see Officer Spencer please?"

"Spencer is on leave. Please sit down. You will be called. You will have to wait."

"All right."

Anne gave her passport and sat down. The wooden bench was hard and without a back. A woman was sitting beside her. Her hair was dishevelled, and she was dabbing her red eyes and sighing. She was accompanied by an elderly man, who was at times putting his hand on her shoulder to bring her some comfort, though she seemed not to notice. No one was apparently concerned about them. From time to time, an officer passed, put a document on a desk without saying a word and went back to duty somewhere.

Several long minutes passed by. Anne was striving to control her mind and to force it to be inactive. To keep her mind absolutely empty was a matter of survival at that moment, maybe the only one.

"Mrs. Anne Standfort?"

"Yes."

"This way, please."

Anne entered a room without windows and was invited to sit down.

"It is a case of an unexplained disappearance, is that right?"

"Yes, my brother..."

"How old is he?"

"He is 37."

"Is he in full possession of all his mental faculties?"

"Absolutely!"

"So what...a family argument?"

"Absolutely not!"

"Would you please explain more clearly?"

Anne complied and gave, as calmly as possible, the explanations that were needed. Her brother and she were in Elberton on a trip. She wanted to use their stay in Elberton to meet someone for whom she was going to write a book. That was her reason for leaving her brother alone at the hotel the previous day in the afternoon and again this morning. They had planned to meet at two o'clock, eat together, and then prepare for their departure. It was thus completely abnormal that he was not in the hotel when she had come back. She had left him at eight forty-five in very good shape, having no other plan but to walk in the park, waiting for her return. They had planned to return to Switzerland the next day.

"Did your brother know anyone in the vicinity of Elberton?"

"No, he did not know anyone."

"You say that his luggage was no longer in his room?"

"Yes. Everything has disappeared—his suitcase, his clothes, his toothbrush—everything."

"Madam, are you sure that you told me the whole story?"

"Of course, I did. You don't believe me?"

"If your brother is in perfect physical and mental health and left the hotel with his luggage, that leads me to think either of a family argument or of a fortuitous encounter."

"What about the key of his room? He would leave with the key of his room?"

"He just forgot…"

"I believe that there is no point in playing this game, sir. I know my brother, and I'm telling you that this disappearance is abnormal. I'm asking you to issue a missing person report, and I want to know what you intend to do!"

"In a case like this, where we are talking about a responsible adult, I suggest that we wait for forty-eight hours. If your brother has not reappeared by then, we will issue a missing person report. In the meantime, return to your hotel, enjoy this beautiful sunshine, calm down, and walk around. Lake Russell is beautiful in this season, and I am sure that your missing brother will come back, ashamed, in a day or two."

Anne stood up, took her passport, and left without a word. Everything was taking place as she had expected. Her story simply made people smile.

She took the road to the hotel, got confirmation that John was not back, went to her room, and lay down on her bed.

Something told her John was dead, that something terrible had taken place, and that there was no going back. "They" had taken John, taking advantage of her absence. They had killed him and had made him disappear. This was becoming blatantly obvious with every second passing by. Perhaps they had been followed since Ingolstadt or perhaps since their departure for Elberton. John's presence had probably annoyed these "gentlemen." The unknown superior had mentioned something, saying that he would not outlive this adventure. There was something implacably coherent to all that. At the same time, she was totally convinced that she was not facing any danger right now. Without being able to explain why, she had the feeling that they would not hurt her. She would write the book, this famous book that would not please everyone. This she understood very well. But who knew what would happen after the book was written? Would they take extreme measures to stop the release of the book? The danger would then surface, for her and for her household. Whatever the cost, she had to call the unknown superior.

"Am I disturbing you?"

"No, Anne, you are not disturbing me. What may I do for you?"

"John, my brother, has disappeared!"

"What are you talking about, Anne? I don't understand you."

"Excuse me, I didn't tell you, but my brother accompanied me to Elberton. He stayed in the hotel during our meetings, and when I returned a little while ago, he had disappeared. His room was empty. I am afraid..."

There was a long silence; Anne could hear the old man breathing.

"Say something!" she shouted.

"Why didn't you inform me?"

"I don't know."

"I know the reason; it is because you don't trust me."

"Perhaps...but it is too late now. What can we do?"

Another moment of silence.

"I am also afraid, my dear; afraid that it is too late for me to do anything about it. If you had told me about your brother, I would have done things accordingly, but in this case..."

Anne shouted, "You are telling me that my brother has been suppressed by your henchmen?"

"Anne, they are not my henchmen, as you call them, but I fear that they deemed it necessary to get rid of someone whose presence was neither expected, nor wanted. Oh, Anne, why didn't you tell me?"

Anne, unable to answer, could not hold her tears back. "It's entirely my fault. He died because of me."

"Don't give in to guilt; it is useless. This is all the more disastrous, it was not necessary for your brother to accompany you as you were not facing any danger."

"What should I do? What should I do? Can you tell me?"

"What I can tell you is how much I regret what just happened. Believe me, I beg you, I had nothing to do with it, Anne. Now you have to go back home, get a grip on yourself, mourn your brother, and let him go. Then I shall contact you. We still need to talk."

"And if I told you that it's over for me?"

"I have not chosen you only for your literary talents but also because you keep your promises. On this point, I am never mistaken!"

"That's easy for you to say!"

"Don't believe that! I am extremely touched by what has happened to you, and once again, if I had been informed, nothing would have taken place."

"I have to inform my husband."

"Of course. May I count on you to urge him to remain calm? I shall give you all the details for our next meeting."

*

Following the phone call with the unknown superior, Anne surprised herself by doing ridiculous things. She looked out the window, watching people leaving the hotel, loaded with suitcases and scolding their rowdy children. She went to the bathroom and combed her hair. A profound conviction entered her mind at that very moment. Never again would she have moments of such intensity in all her life. A bond was broken, and the guilt would stay with her forever.

She called Hans.

"Anne! Are you all right?" The anxious voice of her husband reminded her that it was well past midnight in Basel.

"Excuse me for waking you up."

"Is everything all right, darling?"

Anne burst into tears. "Hans, John has disappeared."

"Disappeared? But, Anne, how is that possible? Explain everything to me."

Once again, she summed up the recent events. Hans listened without interrupting her.

"It's all my fault, isn't it?"

"No, Anne. Your brother is a responsible person. When he made the decision to go with you, I have no doubt that he calculated the risks. There is no point in adding a feeling of guilt on top of your grief. Now the only thing to do is to jump in the first airplane and come back home."

"I can't do that. I have to wait for the missing person report to be filed, which won't be until the day after tomorrow!"

"Anne! Please don't lie to yourself! If the police find anything out, you will be informed. Do you really believe that if John were still alive, he would not have moved heaven and earth so that you wouldn't worry?"

"You're right."

"So, darling, either John is locked up somewhere and his kidnappers will release him only when this whole story is over or—and I don't want you to lose hope, but this is what I believe—we shall not see him again. You got involved in something without seeing the danger, darling, and I remind you that you still have a husband and a son who need you. Therefore, be courageous, as I know you can be, look at the truth, and accept it. Above all, come back immediately!" This last sentence brooked no reply.

"All right. I take the first available flight."

"I love you, Anne."

"I love you too. Don't say anything to Nicolas."

"Of course not."

*

The return trip was a heavy burden for Anne. She had the impression of abandoning her brother for good, despite her feeling that the situation was irreversible.

Hans was waiting for her at the Basel airport. When he saw her devastated face, he had no other reaction than to take her in his arms. They came back without a word. Nicolas would be back from school, joyful as usual, and she would need to adjust.

"Would you like me to prepare a bath for you?"

"Yes, that is kind of you. I must put on a good face for Nicolas.

"Yes, I think that is necessary."

They spent a peaceful evening. Nicolas was joyful but seemed disturbed. Anne explained that the journey had been tiring, and the cuddling did the rest.

When Nicolas was tucked away in bed, Hans drank a glass of whisky, offered some to Anne, who declined, and told her, "Are you aware of your obligation to stop this work immediately, Anne?"

"I am above all aware of the word I gave, Hans. I have informed the unknown superior. I knew that he was not involved in it, and he confirmed it to me. Moreover, if I want to understand what happened, I must follow this all the way to the end. I have not yet said my final word, and I shall avenge my brother!"

"Where do you get this idea of revenge from? First of all, it is useless. And it is not like you to think this way."

"It is also not like me to be the cause of my brother's death. Things no longer look the same, Hans."

"No, indeed."

"Will you help me?"

"No!" Hans's answer was as sharp as a knife.

"I thought I could count on you."

"There are limits to what one may ask in the name of love."

"I am tired."

"I know, but I cannot believe that you can jeopardize your household without a blink of the eye. Anne, tell me that this is not true. Otherwise, I shall believe that our vows no longer have any meaning to you, as well as all our commitments to Nicolas!"

"I shall write this book, I shall understand the mechanisms that underpin these organizations, and perhaps I shall save lives. In my own way, I shall avenge my brother so his death will not have been in vain."

"What about us?"

"I thought that you would understand me."

"Not only do I not understand you, but I cannot accept your decision. You are playing with our lives!"

"In that case, it is your decision."

Hans was furious. Anne stood up and went to him. He exploded. "Oh, please! There is not a time for kissing but for facing our responsibilities, and you apparently don't feel like doing it!"

Without insisting, she went to bed. He did not join her.

The next day, she had a message from the unknown superior, arranging an appointment in Venice on Saturday, October 9. As with her first trip to Venice, somebody would be waiting for her.

Chapter 6

When the old man entered the large room where they had previously met, Anne noted that he looked more bent on his cane, as if, within just a few days, he had become several years older. He came to her, holding out his hand, and at one moment, she thought that he would hug her. He seemed to be on the point of doing it but shyly pulled back, going no further.

"My dear, dear Anne, how are you doing?"

"I am not well at all, are you surprised?"

"How did your husband react?"

"He is demanding that I end our collaboration."

"It was to be expected. It is normal. What have you decided?"

"I am continuing. It is the only way for me to understand and perhaps to prevent other people from falling into the same trap."

"There was initially no trap, Anne, I swear. I have never had any bad intentions toward you."

"I know. You told me clearly and I believe you. The result is the same, nevertheless. My brother is dead, I am now convinced of it, and I have only one hope left, which is revenge."

"Revenge is pointless, Anne. On the other hand, what will be useful will be your book, which will denounce these practices and will reveal the truth."

"I shall write your book; you can count on me. It is all that is left to me. I lost my brother, my husband is becoming distant, and my son might be deeply disturbed. Look at my beautiful life! So, please, give me the information that you still have to give and let us make this meeting as brief as possible. But, first, I want you to answer with complete frankness the question I asked earlier and you skillfully eluded—why did you choose me? I am a professional, but I am not the only one. I also keep my word, but how did you know that? I want to understand, and I want your explanation now, before I can go any further."

"That is your right, and I shall thus explain it to you. I have done research on your ancestors, Anne. I have already mentioned the importance of lineage for people like us, and you are relative of Diana Vaughan through her mother, who was French. You were, therefore, the right person. Moreover, ever since I met you, there has never been a moment's doubt that I made the right choice. You are worthy, just as Diana was, to denounce what has to be denounced. What I put in your hands is much more than a job. It really is a mission. Are you satisfied by this explanation?"

"When I try to think like you do, it is acceptable."

"I am delighted that your mind is at rest. The next event I would like you to attend is the Bilderberg meeting. Here is the list of participants that you will meet. Socialize with them, ask them questions, if you wish. You will then have yet more proof that my information is exact."

"How shall I introduce myself? With what title?"

"You won't have any title. Just wear this ring."

He took a blue velvet case out of his pocket. The ring inside was engraved with the outline of a dove holding an olive branch in its beak. He put the ring on Anne's finger, where it fit perfectly.

"Look! It fits! It is the dove signet ring. Its origin goes back to Illuminism. It is given to women who have been initiated to the secrets of Palladism and represents a powerful Masonic symbol."

"Just wearing this ring will be enough?"

"Yes. It will be enough for all the initiates to know that you are one of us. From that moment on, you will become a VIP, of sorts—doors opened to you and everything made possible. And later on, I shall show you a few simple signs of Masonic identification that you will memorize. Finally, I allowed myself, in light of the circumstances, to organize your trip. Your air tickets are reserved, and you will have a splendid room in the Dolce Sitges, located south of Barcelona, where the conference will take place. In this season, you will have splendid weather. The fall season is impressive in Spain."

"Do you really believe that I shall be able to appreciate the weather?"

"No, you won't, I know, but even so...in any case, I shall have some solace knowing that you will enjoy the sun of Catalonia."

"All right, everything is in proper order then."

"Please, Anne, I still have something important to ask you. I would like to explain in greater detail what triggered my desire for this book. When it is written, as I already told you, you will have to distribute the book. I shall probably not be here anymore. But I would like you to carry a more faithful memory of the person I really am. This is not about narcissism, I assure you—and even more so in light of what has recently taken place. I want to leave in your memory a trace of my redemption. I cannot leave this world if I know that you curse me."

"First of all, I have no feeling of hatred against you, and secondly you don't need to justify yourself in front of me."

"I insist." Again, he seemed to be crushed by a heavy burden of sadness. "First of all, my dear, and even if you don't have much appetite right now, I had a special snack prepared for you."

"It is useless. I can't swallow anything."

"I know that, and that is why I have chosen a delicacy that can be taken without feeling any hunger. You should not neglect your health, Anne. Life goes on."

"Oh, please. Spare me your platitudes."

"A platitude it is indeed, but it is also an inescapable reality. Come, everything is ready."

When she had entered the room, Anne had not paid attention to the table set at an angle. It was covered with a lace tablecloth, and placed upon it were silver-gilt forks and knives and two cups of crystal containing a splendid lobster salad.

"You will take a glass of Pouilly Fumé?"

"How do you know that I like this? Ah! I see that surveillance is not always bad."

"You said it with a smile! I thus forget the bitterness of your deduction."

They ate silently. Anne was young, full of life. Since lobster was her favorite dish, she could not resist the temptation.

When coffee was served, they went back to the living room, and when they were comfortably sitting in armchairs, he started to talk again.

"If you will forgive me, I shall talk a lot about myself, but this will be the only meeting where I will be the focus of your attention. I have been living, as you probably guessed, in extreme luxury without ever wondering why, but I have no childhood memories. In our world, children lack nothing. They wear expensive clothes, have sophisticated toys, and are served by an army of governesses and preceptors. Their fathers are absent. Their mothers are always soft and lovely, all the more so because they see their dear ones only when they are freshly washed and in their pyjamas, shortly before going to bed, for a session of kisses, which are often absentminded. Forgive me, I should not generalize. In some families, there are surely mothers who are present and attentive, but that was not my experience."

He shifted in his chair and continued. "And then they grow, travel for their studies, and at last really start a well-planned existence with the goal of achieving success, which is actually guaranteed. This is all normal, and there is nothing so ecstatic about all that. As long as the rules are observed, life goes on without trouble. People marry according to the instructions they receive. We multiply children as we multiply money. This money is properly managed in order to yield fruit. That's how things are. Life goes on, year after year, and the end always justifies the means. There is only one path, and it is the good one. It is unacceptable to pose questions or to consider another order of things. I was like all those who came before me, working to establish a new world conforming to Palladism, and that was my life until August 12, 2010. This was the date when I reached, without searching for it, the fifth level of conscience."

"The fifth level of conscience?"

"Yes, I have done research in order to understand what happened to me, and the conclusion was obvious. Until that time, like billions of people, I was living like a kind of robot, reproducing the thoughts and deeds that had been dictated to me. But on that day—which was not a special day, and I was absolutely not expecting this—I suddenly had some kind of illumination. This was not a physical disease. I was carried by a vibration from another dimension, and I was suddenly aware of what my life had been. I noticed for the first time the refined luxury of my gorgeous office surrounding me. I kept talking to a collaborator, but I was split in a dual personality. My speech and the orders I was giving were coherent, but I was somewhere else. I don't know what excuse I found to end the conversation, but I took refuge in a storage room. Can you imagine that, Anne? A storage room!"

These remnants of snobbishness made Anne smile internally.

"If someone was looking for me, I was confident that this place would not be visited. Being short of breath, I leaned against a shelf and I saw my life: the life of a villain, of a man with no heart and no honour. As I said earlier, survival of the fittest is always the best law for those who hold power, and I had spent most of my time using this law without shame. Might Makes Right was my motto. Suddenly, alone in this tiny, dusty room, I felt in complete despair. Then, in just a second, I was soaking with sweat. It was as if huge amounts of hot water had been poured inside me, and this sweat was the symbol of my abjection. I wanted to think of my children. Yes, I remembered that I had children, but how many? I did not know if I had four or five. They were all adults, of course, but what about their ages? And the dates of their birthdays? And the woman who had given birth to them to me? No one was lacking anything in my splendid residence, built according to my plans by the best workers. I remember them using a plumb level. Then I wondered, what is a plumb level by the way? Oh, yes! It is an instrument to check if what one has built is straight. What I had built was not straight! I could see right in front of me the scope of all my misdeeds. I had money, so much money that spending it was just exhausting and boring. I had recently turned seventy years old. I spent these seventy miserable years not giving any happiness to anyone. I was useless for seventy years. I had offered a lot of reflection, intelligence, expertise, and strategy. I had given orders, which were brief and without appeal. I had given many orders and no love. I had been the patron of numerous provocative artists because their style matched Palladism but have never felt any emotion for a painting, and music bores me stiff. At that moment, my knees buckled and I fell and wept. The words that pierced my brain were *too late*—too late to change, too late to return. I had no hope to be able to make amends for my errors. I was about to die soon. I was about to go through the tunnel. Those who have come back say that it is a tunnel of light, but mine would be black. And I became aware of what I would leave behind me, of the image that would remain in the mind of my children, the image of a harsh and inflexible man. I was the man whose statements were as sharp as knives and in front of whom one should bow down. I was a stiff-necked man, feared by many, a man who had a record of bringing ruin and, who knows, perhaps caused one or two suicides of poor people who had failed in business. The father who never hugged, who never told stories in the evening before the children go to bed, who could not bear noise and, even less, the sound of laughter. And it is in this attitude of despair but also of humility that I reached, I believe, the sixth level of conscience. This is where my ego disappeared. At this level, there remains only a soul, which is beaming with love and humanity and ready to merge with the universal spirit. My tears were still flowing, seventy years of repressed tears, and yet I was invaded by a wordless emotion close to happiness. In order to guide me toward this state of grace, I needed someone to love me, beyond earthly love. This could only be God, therefore! In a daze, I thought I heard a voice, which told me, 'Is God not precisely for that?' Thus we have come full circle, all is in all. God is in me, and I am in Him. We are simply one. He needs me, I need him, and everything remains possible. These are the things, Anne, that I wanted to share with you. I have been a bad person throughout my life. First, it was unconscious because I was a child and I found justifications for everything; later, it was to resemble my peers, to be part of the clan, to follow its beliefs. It took me all these years before the truth could illuminate me. Forgive me if I bore you, but I wanted you to know who I am becoming."

"It's good that you shared this with me. I understand you, and I admire you. Your conversion is amazing, and what you are doing is courageous. We are always sort of victims of our education and background, and it may take time before we open our eyes. But you accepted it, you faced it, and that is good. My brother too is a victim of his education. In our world of the 'dominated,' a brother sacrifices himself for his sister, and love has precedence over money. Therefore, I would like you to know that I shall not write your book because of the money you gave me. I don't yet know what I shall do with this money once the expenses for the publication have been paid. I might decide to give it to charity. Or I could go to Ethiopia and build a school there, or I could sue companies that claim to fight starvation with harmful products. I shall see. But I shall withdraw the money from the bank and shall spend it to the last cent in order to bring education and well-being to those who need it the most. You can be sure of that."

"You are the right person in the right job, Anne."

"Now, with your permission, I shall go back home and try to patch things up with my husband."

"You will surely manage to do this."

Again Anne had the feeling that the old man was trying to approach her. She held out her two hands, and he took them between his hands and kissed each of them.

Chapter 7

Shin left Karl's office in a state of indescribable fury. How could this fat know-it-all call him a good-for-nothing? Was he responsible for the congenital stupidity of the colleagues who had been imposed on him? Did Karl imagine that the elimination of a six-foot-tall guy at nine o'clock in the morning in a busy hotel had been a piece of cake? Of course they had taken some risks, but they had ultimately done very well. No one would ever find the body in the building site where they had buried it, and it would soon become impossible to actually identify the body. Wasn't that the main thing? And now, Karl was angry because of that letter found in the kid's room in Basel. What was so important about this letter? In any case, he had now firmly made up his mind: one more incident of this kind would push him to offer his services elsewhere. He possessed all the addresses of Karl's friends, and he knew that some of them would be happy to hire him. This thought eased his mind, and he left the building whistling.

*

Meanwhile, Karl, having scolded the young Korean, was almost in a good mood as he made a few useful telephone calls. The message was short: Mr. Robert "Y" was indeed drifting toward betrayal. The fool had changed sides. Who knows, his stupid "redemption" might have been caused by the pretty, blonde journalist.

In any case, his fate was sealed; he had put his signature on the ridiculous letter revealing everything. One word, only one, was necessary. He had indicated he was a *former* unknown superior. No further comment was necessary, and he would pay for his misdeed according to the law of their milieu.

Karl's last call was to Shin.

"You are useless, but I need you. This is important, so note this down. First, a not-so-young lady will be needed."

"What for?"

"To take care of a child for two days."

"Ah, a kidnapping. What age?"

"Twelve years old."

"OK, I have the person. Where?"

"Basel."

"The Standfort son?"

"Yes."

"What date?"

"On October 28, when he leaves school. I imagine that it will be around four o'clock, but you will have to get information on the school and bus schedule. Ideally, you should have about one hour before the parents may notice that the child is missing."

"No problem."

"Very good. I want the child to be in perfect condition for October 31. Feed him well and take a change of clothes. Also take a television set and games."

"The apartment is equipped."

"Reserve your tickets. I want to see the child in good shape on the thirty-first in Jerusalem."

"All right."

"No mistakes, this time! I'm counting on you."

"Mistakes never happen when I select my colleagues myself!"

"Yes, all right. I want a report immediately!"

"Of course."

The conversation ended, as always, with the uninviting click of the telephone.

*

On this October 14, as announced, Barcelona was beaming under a gorgeous autumn sun. Anne could not ignore it. The air had a fragrance of carelessness. She breathed it deeply, and for the first time in many hours and days, she surprised herself by smiling.

The hotel was majestic and her room luxurious, exactly as the old man had announced. Their last meeting was engraved in her memory, and his speech had deeply touched her. Victim of his education and background, he was probably deeply suffering at that moment and, undoubtedly, expecting this death that he said was scheduled. She had understood that the disappearance of John had shocked him and that his regrets were absolutely sincere. Without a shadow of resentment, she felt only compassion for him now.

Concerning Hans, his position was clear. In front of Nicolas, he kept up appearances. But when they were alone, their separation was complete. Anne was deeply hurt. From their first encounter until her return from Elberton, they had been so happy together. They had had some disagreements at times, but nothing serious had ever taken place. She fervently believed in their love. But it had taken only one serious disagreement and all of a sudden he had turned away, leaving her alone with her guilt and an awful feeling of responsibility, not only in relation to John but also to those who needed to know the truth. She had believed that Hans was strong, but he behaved like a deserter. On top of her grief, she felt terribly disappointed.

Upon leaving Nicolas, she had felt his hidden anxiety. She had tried to reassure him with smiles and cuddles, but knowing her son, who was smart and intuitive, it would be difficult to hide the reality for long.

Despite all these dark thoughts in her mind, she decided to go out. She had been told about a good local restaurant named Los Caracoles, and having eaten nothing during the day, she felt hungry. It was located near the Rambla, and when the taxi dropped her off, she was immediately charmed by this great and beautiful avenue lined with trees, a kind of promenade where she saw that tourists as well as the local people liked to walk. And as she walked, striding along the small adjacent streets, she came across Los Caracoles. She thought that she would first sit at a table on the terrace for an aperitif and then go in the restaurant. Sitting in the sun, letting it warm her with her eyes closed, she hoped to call back her lost carefree life and tried to force her mind to be inactive, but in vain. She drank small sips of a delicious sangria and took pleasure in feeling the warmth of the alcohol moving through her body. The melancholy gave way to a fleeting peace, and she entered the restaurant with a smile.

"Tapas, senora?"

"Sorry?"

"Ah, you speak English? Me too!" The waiter explained to her that she had a choice. She could either eat only tapas, a variety of small dishes served at the bar, or go to a table on the first floor for a menu. She decided to stay at the bar, where she could choose among the several dishes offered to her. She found herself facing a dozen small dishes. She had no idea what they were made of, but she found them delicious. She also had a small carafe of "tinto," which was suggested to her.

She was in a world that was unreal and peaceful. Nobody wanted to harm her; people loved her. There was no pain in this world, for the time being, in this particular place, where people were talking and laughing loudly. She ate the food and drank the wine, and then she went out. The sun had not yet set. She wandered along the Rambla for some time. When she took a taxi to go back to the hotel, she noticed that tears had been running down her face, probably for quite some time.

She tossed and turned during the night with a succession of nightmares, leaving a vague, strange feeling in her heart. She was scared when she saw her face. She felt that she had aged ten years in a few weeks, and it was high time that she react. She knew that guilt is a paralyzing condition, lowering a person's energy to its lowest level and preventing him or her from going forward. John would be in her thoughts the rest of her life, and Nicolas needed a peaceful and positive mother. Hans's behavior, on the other hand, made her sorrowful, and she was increasingly disappointed. Every day, she was waiting for a sign or a hand to be offered, but the door seemed to be forever shut. She sometimes thought that if this attitude was to indicate a deliberate rejection, it would then be necessary to consider that the love he had sworn to her was actually very shallow. "For the best" had, of course, never been jeopardized, but "for the worse" was greatly so. "Wait and see" seemed to be the only intelligent behavior.

*

With comfortable clothes and shoes on, she went down to have her breakfast. Since a day of freedom had somehow been imposed on her by the unknown superior, she decided to spend it visiting the city. Without having any precise plan, she chose to go to Güell Park, and she tasted the shy sunshine, which was caressing the agaves on this October morning. She at last saw the works of Gaudi—particularly his chimneys, which a couple of friends had mentioned enthusiastically, and the Casa Batlló, with its amazing facade and surroundings. Then she decided to contemplate the panorama of the city at the Gran Plaça Circular. Having fun with her nonsensical itinerary, she jumped from one taxi to the next with carelessness. It was close to two o'clock when she decided to eat in a small tapas bar.

Then, since the sun had not capitulated, she went to the zoological garden, whose reputation went beyond Spanish borders, but that was a bad idea. Seeing the animals in cages did not bring her any peace. She immediately drew a parallel with her situation and clearly saw how much she was also deprived of freedom. On top of this demoralizing thought, there was the fact that her acceptance of the money had triggered the whole process. No one had forced her. Another option would have been to refuse, stand up, and turn her back on this banker. She had done none of these things. Today, trapped by her attitude, she had to go all the way. She quickly came out of the garden and decided to walk toward the Sagrada Familia.

The magnificent cathedral welcomed her in the glistening of its sublime stained glass windows. She sat down on a low chair and let the silence give her some relief. Outside, the shadows were progressively finding their positions. She wanted to watch the sea, and she walked for quite some time, turning her thoughts over and over.

Why were these families rich beyond anything one might imagine? It is because they have been using and abusing the mechanism of interest-bearing loans for more than ten generations? These people maintain and develop beliefs that are beyond acceptable limits. With the power of their money and their beliefs, they stand on a deeply rooted racist and a eugenic philosophy. For them, this is the most normal way of seeing the future of the world. To achieve their goal, they must remodel the world to fit their image. Therefore, their action plan is carefully mapped out. Convinced of their natural superiority, they have chosen the option of eliminating those who aren't useful to them. The "flunkys" will be spared as long as they do not think.

The sun had long since gone down when she realized that she was still far away from the sea. She changed her mind and called a taxi to take her back to the hotel. Tomorrow would again be a day, Anne knew, during which she would be confronted by values she found offensive. She was no longer afraid, knowing that she was not in danger, but the knowledge of their objectives and their manipulation to fulfil those goals made her blood run cold. She would have to face that, and she would probably have to go so far as to play along with them. She would do what was necessary.

*

On October 16, she woke up at six o'clock and was ready to go well before nine. She was going to take part in this famous, secret Bilderberg meeting! According to the information that she had been able to put together, it was officially a yearly gathering of about 130 VIPs from Europe and the United States. Various organized sessions were aimed at the promotion of a global world. This global world would be governed, ideally, not by elected politicians but by businessmen, and it would be run like a major multinational company because this management was deemed the most efficient.

The conferences take place in huge hotels entirely reserved for the occasion and severely guarded by the police. The first of these gatherings was organized in the Netherlands, in the Bilderberg Hotel in 1954. Among the founders, one could find the banker D. Rockefeller and Prince Bernhard of the Netherlands.

Absolutely nothing of what is said in the meetings can leak outside. As a matter of fact, Anne noticed that the hotel was entirely surrounded by security forces. In the distance, protesters were staging a demonstration. They probably would have enjoyed being in Anne's position in order to know what was being decided during this meeting.

Anne knew, however, from the unknown superior, that decisions were generally made somewhere else, at higher levels, and long before the meeting. The main purpose of the meeting was to inform the participants so that they can prepare for the next steps, but it was also to evaluate their reactions, to see if they were ready to put the decisions into practice or if more persuasion needed to be applied. Things were done in this way even though the people attending were well known and influential. Anne, her head spinning and her ring on her finger, felt that she had the soul of a con man when she thought of the role that she would have to play, and she was hoping to be blessed by heaven with the necessary talent just when needed.

The parking lot was the theater of a smooth ballet of limousines, and the lobby was buzzing with greetings and congratulations. She put her badge on the lapel of her suit and headed toward the conference hall. Among the 238 suggested topics were the war against Iran, the climate, and finance. Anne chose the latter.

The lecturer, a certain Paul Greenbern, was a university professor and a special adviser to the American central bank. His lecture was entitled "A world currency in the global world that we wish to establish." Anne took her seat in the conference hall. Professor Greenbern waited until the audience had quieted and then spoke with a loud voice:

Dear friends and participants of the Bilderberg, I am honored to be able to address you as a member of the Trilateral Commission. As most of you already know, the Trilateral Commission is a think tank founded by David Rockefeller as well as by the central bankers Volker and Greenspan. It brings together three to four hundred of the most influential and distinguished people. They are businessmen, politicians, and intellectual decision-makers, of central Europe, North America, and Asia-Pacific. Its goal is to promote and build political and economic cooperation between these three crucial areas of the world, the poles of the triad.

As you may know, the Trilateral Commission was established in 1973, and from the beginning, its publications mentioned the birth of a world currency. You may, for instance, find on our website the major report "Towards a Renovated World Monetary System." We, therefore, have a well-developed expertise in this field, and I am convinced that the current crisis is indeed a fertile soil to see the emergence of this new world currency. This will be the major event at the dawn of this millennium.

Let us first make clear that a world currency does not mean a currency that will replace all others. For instance, the dollar is now assuming the role of a world reserve currency. It is used in international trade, particularly the trade of raw materials. But the fact is that it is the property of the United States. It cannot serve as a currency in every country. On the other hand, a world currency would be issued by a global central bank. It would not be tied to a specific country. It is quite possible that, in the long run, the traditional currencies will disappear. But initially a global common currency would be just another currency with the existing currencies. Keynes called it the bancor. The name does not matter.

Those who defend a world currency do so because they see several advantages. It is impossible to go through all of them. I shall just mention a few. Paul Volcker, the former director of the Fed and currently an advisor to President Obama, gave a good summary of the main advantage when he said, "a global economy requires a global currency." With the existence of a global currency, the central banks of the various countries will not have to keep reserves of currencies to protect their national currency. This would eliminate the risk of the monetary crisis that takes place when one currency is deserted for the benefit of others. This universal currency would eliminate the risk of the competitive devaluation of a national currency at the detriment of others. It would also favor trade, reducing the costs of export businesses, which would no longer be obliged to hedge themselves against the risks of exchange rates. Unlike the existing currencies, the value of a global currency would be fixed by an international standard and not by the law of supply and demand on the currency market. Then, with a global currency, which would be issued by a world central bank, you would not see its value depend on the particular governance of a country, as it is now the case with the American dollar, whose value is threatened by the deficits which the current president is constantly increasing. But I will say no more since I have no doubt that you are already convinced.

The question is now, what could this new currency be like? Let us take the example of the euro, itself a currency created very recently. Let us remember that the euro first existed under the form of the ECU, which was a basket of European currencies. Keep this in mind for a few moments; I shall again talk about it later.

Before that, I would like to talk to you briefly about a kind of currency that has been allocated by the International Monetary

Fund since 1969. That year, the situation on the foreign exchange markets was very tense. The central banks were afraid of not having enough dollars—or gold, which amounted to the same thing at that time—to maintain the exchange rates. It is in this context that the IMF created a sort of new currency: the Special Drawing Rights, or SDR. An SDR is worth 0.88 grams of gold.

The IMF freely distributes a certain number of SDR to each of its members on the basis of their financial contribution to the IMF. A member state may decide to sell its SDR to support its currency. Let us imagine for instance, that following a commercial deficit, the currency of one member state is weakening. The government of this country or its central bank may buy its currency and pay by selling its SDR. In this case, the country selling SDR would have a deficit of SDR, and the country that buys it would have a surplus. The country that sells would then have to pay interest to the country having a surplus of SDR. An SDR is, therefore, a "right to borrow from a consenting lender," a bank reserve on which a country may draw. Like all the present currencies, which are created ex-nihilo, an SDR is backed by the promise of a country that it will honor its debt. If a country is not using its SDR, it does not pay or receive interest.

After the collapse of the Bretton Woods system in 1973, the value of the SDR has been determined in relation to a basket of currencies, which now consists of the American dollar, the euro, the pound sterling, and the yen. The exchange and interest rates of the SDR are published daily on the website of the IMF. See the parallel between the ECU, which was backed by a basket of European currencies, and the SDR, which is also backed by a basket of world currencies. The SDR represents the foundation of a future world currency in its infancy, and the IMF represents the future world central bank.

Professor Greenbern continued his lecture by talking about the substitution account at the IMF, which would allow the major holders of Dollars, Euros, or other important currencies to exchange them against SDR. The IMF would use this money to buy public debt. The explanations were becoming more and more technical, but Anne perceived that this mechanism would facilitate the recycling of the present currencies in a new currency and would reduce the weight of the public debt in the economy. Just before she started to lose track completely, she understood, one more time, that this world central bank would concentrate enormous power in the hands of a minority of people. She remembered the words of the old unknown superior, "Now, in order to solve a problem of overflowing credit, governments borrow even more. For the authorities, the solution is to pile up new debt on dubious debt. It is stupid, but it is exactly what we want because this will create even greater chaos, which will help implement the new world currency. The oligarchic families know perfectly well that there is no way to prevent a total collapse after the explosion of a credit bubble. The president of the American central bank maintained the rates too low much too long after the explosion of the Internet bubble. He was perfectly aware that he would generate a real estate bubble, coupled with new products of securitization, which would be massively issued. It is with our agreement that he was assigned as president of the Fed, and he has been acting in full accord with our plans to trigger the greatest depression of all time. Since the beginning of the crisis, only the banks and the major holders of bonds have really been supported by the taxes paid by the taxpayers. Remember that we lit the fuse, and we know perfectly well that nothing will prevent the crisis from getting worse." The unknown superior was right, and it was the main thing for Anne, who had stopped listening to the lecturer.

She started to observe the faces of the people who were in the audience, and she was amazed to notice that no one expressed any sign of disapproval, any reaction that would express a disagreement or at least a divergent view. Signs of agreement could be seen everywhere, even on certain well-known VIPs and renowned politicians who have strong media coverage, not to mention the prestigious colleagues of the press.

She thus adopted a similar attitude and even appeared to be contemplative. Her arms folded, she managed to make the ring conspicuous on her left hand for the people surrounding her, and she quickly harvested the fruit of her investment. With a few glances and a light smile, they assured her there was no doubt that she was one of them, and even if she had no desire to be one of them, it would be helpful to facilitate contacts. She did not intend to stay in this place longer than necessary, but she thought that it would be useful, in order to be well positioned, to start a conversation with Paul Greenbern, who was surrounded by people as soon as his lecture was over. Everybody was flocking to the lounge, where drinks were being served, and a cloud of groupies was already surrounding him. She would thus have to cut through the crowd and be audacious. She was still six feet from him when she called him with a loud voice: "Your lecture was extremely interesting, dear sir, but I was telling myself that the establishment of a central bank in the United States had already been tedious, so a world central bank..."

He was startled, but he looked at her, came closer, took a discrete glance at the ring Anne was exhibiting, and read what was written on her badge. The groupies faded away. "So, you are a journalist?"

"Yes, I am a journalist, one very interested in finance. So, tell me, how are you going to convince everyone of the necessity of a world central bank?"

"It is true that the birth of the American central bank was difficult, but we managed to do it. It will be the same with a world central bank. The secret is simple: trigger a major world crisis and such financial chaos that the mob will cry out for a solution. With magnanimity, we shall propose a world central bank, and the idiots will shed tears of gratitude. It is exactly what we did in the beginning of the twentieth century in the United States."

"Really? Please tell me more about that."

"You know, for most people, it is a self-evident truth that central banks are needed to regulate monetary markets by intervening on short-term interest rate and on exchange rates. But it was not always the case. As I told you, the birth of the Fed in December 1913 was the object of many hot debates in the early days of the twentieth century. One of the most adamant opponents was Congressman Charles A. Lindbergh, the father of the famous pilot, who openly spoke of 'a legislative crime.' In 1932, Congressman Louis McFadden declared that the banks of the Federal Reserve were private credit monopolies preying on the people of the United States for their own profit as well as for the profit of foreign swindlers! You see, the notion of a central bank was seen very unfavorably by some, who were adamantly attached to the independence of the states and the banks. Can you imagine! Before 1913, in the same country, one could see several kinds of dollars and no central bank. It is now more or less the same situation at the world level, with several currencies and no world central bank. It is unbelievable! Anyway, we managed to do it in 1913, so you understand that I am not afraid of those who criticize our old, ambitious project of a world central bank! But I am becoming emotional. Let me tell you how we did it. In 1907, a report published by the press group of JP Morgan launched a rumor about the financial health of a major bank. There was a bank run, and it was the starting point of a serious financial crisis, which we exploited to convince public opinion of the necessity of a unique dollar managed by a central bank. You know the story?"

"I have heard a little about it, but I would be pleased if you could give me more details."

"Of course! It is a story worth telling, as you will see. From 1907, we regularly launched numerous articles and debates in the newspapers of that time. They stressed the necessity of improving the operation of banking institutions in order to avoid new crises, which were so damaging for the population. In November 1910, the highest financial elite discretely prepared the birth of the Fed, in quite bizarre circumstances, it should be pointed out. To avoid unwanted attention, Senator Nelson Aldrich invited six important figures to secretly meet in his private train in a New Jersey railway station. The press was to remain unaware of this meeting. These people had to arrive separately and pretend not to know one another. The train was to take them on a trip of eight hundred miles, to a hotel belonging to the senator and located on a private island, Jekyll Island. Officially, the purpose of this meeting was a duck hunt! These guests represented more than one-fourth of the world's wealth and regrouped the two "enemy brothers," the Morgans and the Rockefellers. There was to be total discretion and the press was to have no idea that the law giving birth to the Fed had simply been written by the representatives of the major commercial banks of that time. That is why these gentlemen were officially on a hunting trip! Moreover, in order to make things acceptable and hide this cartel, this central bank was to bear the less-centralized name of the Federal Reserve and regroup several Federal Reserve Banks established in various states. It is even funnier when one realizes that a central bank has no reserve. The law introduced by the senator was fiercely debated, but was finally voted and signed by President Wilson on December 23, 1913."

"Well! I understand better your description of quite bizarre!"

"What is more surprising is that this story was revealed only progressively and almost twenty years later, in 1935, in an article written by a banker named F. Vanderlip, one of the participants of the Jekyll Island meeting. What we should keep in mind is that, following a major financial crisis, the highest financial elite within the profession discretely put in place the creation of a central bank and a unique currency in the United States, and this work was accepted by the political world. This time again, we shall use the current crisis as an opportunity to establish our world central bank. You will see—we shall succeed!"

"I could listen to you for hours! But tell me, you who are so well-versed in this matter, how do you see the future? Shall we be able to guide, thanks to this unique world currency, this herd of useless people that we are dragging along behind us?"

"Ah! It is clear that this will not be done with a snap of the fingers. We put up with Africa and support India and Asia, and we will need to make drastic decisions. We have no more time to waste, and our vision is clear. Fortunately, we do have a range of possibilities..."

Anne, with great effort, offered him a fake smile and shook his hand according to the Masonic rules. Forcing herself even further, she put some warmth in it, which she wasn't sure she could do. The lectures were to start again, and she left—or, more precisely, escaped—the place. She appreciated again her comfortable hotel room, went to the terrace, put a shawl around her shoulders, and tried to find solace from the last beams of a tired sun partially covered by clouds. It was around noon and she decided to fly back home immediately.

*

As soon as she had inserted the key in the lock of her apartment, she heard Nicolas screaming "Mummy!" She had sent a message to Hans in order to inform him of her time of arrival, but as she had expected, he was not waiting for her at the airport. He watched her come in and kissed her politely on the cheek.

"I shall be away for the rest of the weekend," he informed her.

"Ah? And where are you going?"

"This is of interest to you?"

"Oh, Hans, is it really necessary to be so aggressive?"

"You will allow me not to answer this question. You have a message asking for your presence in Venice tomorrow, but you will have to postpone the date. You must stay with Nicolas since I must leave now and shall not be back until Sunday evening."

"All right, Hans. I shall take care of it."

"So be it." The door was already closed.

"Mummy, what is the matter with you and Dad? Are you angry with each other?"

"A little, my darling, but don't worry. It will not last."

"But why? I have never seen him like this."

"Me neither. But it is also the first time that my work has made him so upset. You need to understand him: I often go away, and he often has to deal with everything on top of his work at the bank. It is too much for him, and that is normal. But very soon everything will be OK."

"Mummy, I should tell you something serious."

"Something serious, my darling! What is it?"

Nicolas was obviously very embarrassed.

"Please, come with me. We shall sit comfortably on the sofa and have a big, big hug and you will tell me everything."

Nicolas curled up against his mother, sniffed, and launched himself. "Do you remember the letter?"

"Which letter?"

"The letter from Russia, with the beautiful stamps you gave me."

"Oh! Yes, I do remember that."

"Dad threw it in the trash."

"Did he? I don't remember."

"Well, I took the letter from the dustbin and showed it to Uncle John."

Anne turned pale. "Why did you show it to Uncle John?"

"Because *he* knows everything."

"And what did he tell you?"

"He told me to be careful and to tell you if I saw anything abnormal."

"Have you seen anything abnormal, then?"

"Yes! One evening, I wanted to look at that letter in my desk and it wasn't there anymore. I knew that was going to happen!"

Again, she felt some difficulty breathing, but she absolutely couldn't let Nicolas see how troubled she was. "Are you sure about this, my darling?"

"Yes, Mummy, I am sure. I am very tidy, as you know. It was in the drawer, just above my stamp collection. I really knew this would happen!"

"When did you notice that it had disappeared?"

"That was the day when you came back from your trip to Germany with Uncle John.

"Did you mention this to him?"

"Yes, of course. I went to do my homework in my bedroom before dinner. When I saw that the letter was no longer there, I called him, supposedly to see my drawings, and I told him. I could see that he felt uneasy about it, he again told me to take care of you and to inform you if I saw something strange."

"Did you talk to Dad about that?"

"No. He had put the letter in the trash, and he would not have been happy that I took it out."

"Quite likely, indeed. By the way, I suggest that you don't talk to him about all that. He has got enough troubles for the moment."

"Mummy, is it serious?"

"No, my darling, it is not serious. All of this concerns the work that I am doing for a very old man. He wants me to write a book for him, and he has much information to give me. That is the reason why I often have to travel. But soon the task of writing will start, and then I shall be at home all the time. Things will get back to normal. You will see."

"What about Uncle John, Mummy? When shall we see him?"

"Not for a while, my sweetheart. He will be traveling for a few months."

"For a few months! That's too long. I would like to see him."

"You have to be patient, my darling. Now, let's go to the pizzeria nearby. We can buy a warm pizza for dinner, and tomorrow I shall take you to the restaurant and we shall eat the kind of fondue that you like, all right?"

"Yes, all right. But Dad said that everything we need is in the fridge."

"Well, that doesn't help me because it is already late and I don't want to do any cooking.

Give me a little time before we go; I want to check my e-mail."

"May I watch television?"

Anne gave her permission and, repressing a painful smile, went to the computer. Indeed, the unknown superior was expressing his wish to see her on Sunday, but he did apologize for being so demanding. She forgot that John already told her that her computer had likely been hacked and answered that she would have come on Sunday, but could not since her husband would be absent until Sunday evening. However, on Monday, if there were flights available, it would not be a problem. She added that, even though they would see each other soon, she thought it necessary to inform him that his introductory letter, which she had believed to be destroyed, had been recovered by her son without her knowledge and had now mysteriously gone missing. This was yet another proof that her apartment had been searched. Her private life was no longer her own. She saw that as an invasion of privacy that could not be underestimated.

Fifteen minutes later, she received an answer. He understood that she would not be able to come on Sunday but begged her to come as soon as possible. They had to talk. The airport would be informed, and a return ticket in her name would be reserved on Monday.

The evening was peaceful. Nicolas seemed to have forgotten his fears, they watched a television program together after dinner, and he peacefully went to bed. The next day, Anne dedicated herself completely to her son, checked his laundry, and carefully went through his notebooks and homework. Then, as scheduled, they went to eat a delicious fondue in Nicolas' favorite restaurant and then walked for a long time. Nicolas had taken his roller skates and took the opportunity to show off in front of his mother. They came back tired and happy.

When they returned home, Hans was already there, sitting on the sofa, straight and stiff as a board. His hands were on his knees, and he stared straight ahead.

"Oh!" Anne exclaimed. "I thought you would come back later."

"Am I back too early? I can leave if you want."

"Hans, this is not what I meant! I am happy that you are here. We shall have dinner together."

"Excuse me for being rude."

Anne went and sat beside her husband, taking his arm and putting it around her shoulders. Watching the scene, Nicolas came to sit down, half on the knees of his dad, half on the knees of his mother. Everything in his attitude showed his need to rediscover his parents and the usual atmosphere of their life, and they understood that they needed to give him this comfort. Hans leaned back against the sofa, and Anne felt that he was relaxing. She suddenly realized how many things he had had to face and how demanding she had been, and her resentment melted in a second. She felt a little bit ashamed and took the risk of kissing him; he did not shy away.

After dinner Nicolas allowed himself to ask for additional cuddling. They could respond to that with no reluctance, and it was a providential truce.

When Nicolas was asleep and they met again in the living room, each sitting in a different armchair, Hans resumed the discussion: "So, now, what is the plan?"

"My love, please, let us not destroy the peace we have just built. This is a difficult time for you, and I am aware of that. It is tragic for me that I lost my brother because of my mistake, and seeing you become distant with me only complicates things further."

"I am not becoming distant, Anne, but I remain critical of your attitude. I still do not understand why you insist on working for this crook."

"Hans, he is not a crook, I swear. He is a devastated person who is sorry for what he has done in his life and who wants to denounce unacceptable practices. I want to help him do that, and in so doing I would like to redeem John's sacrifice, if possible. We are coming close to the end of this ordeal. I still have to go to San Francisco to attend a meeting of the Bohemian Club, which will take two or three days, but I absolutely refused to go to the event on October 31."

"What about Venice? You do have to go to Venice, right?"

"Yes, tomorrow, but for the last time. Then I will have all the information I need and I can start writing. From that moment, I shall not leave you any more for quite some time. Are you with me, Hans?"

Hans took a long time to think. He put his hand over his eyes, as if trying to erase a painful vision. Anne was overwhelmed and saw that he was crying.

"Anne, I appreciated your brother. Yes, I had great esteem for him, and above all, I liked him. We both knew that. Our small verbal fights were just a game, and when he offered to go with you, I accepted wholeheartedly because I felt reassured. I am therefore as responsible as you are. I had doubts about the purpose of this affair, and I just stood by."

"My darling, I should also confess to you the reason I accepted this work. Of course, there was the oddness of the situation—the letter from Russia, the bank, the trip to Venice. But also there was the amount put on that account, and I should admit that I was impressed by it."

"The forty thousand francs?"

"It was not forty thousand francs, Hans, but four hundred million francs."

"What are you saying?"

"Four hundred million francs. If I lied on the exact figure, it is because I knew that you would not take it and that perhaps you would force me to give it back."

Hans had put his hands over his eyes, as if to refuse an unbearable reality. After a while, he continued. "Indeed, you can be sure that I would have forced you to give it back!"

"On the spot, I had the conviction that money had not been my only motivation, but if I think more deeply about it, I see clearly my responsibility. The old man offered this astronomical amount as proof that his wealth had no limits. But I learned that the director of the bank had immediately informed the other families. Surprised and worried, they got interested in me. By accepting this amount, I got involved, and I cannot go back. Believe me, I signed as if I was pushed by an invisible force. I did not think about the consequences, and I still don't understand what happened to me."

"You are caught in a trap, Anne; the three of us are caught in a trap."

"No, not at all! For me, yes, I should write the book, but you and Nicolas have nothing to do with this work!"

"And John? Did he have anything to do with your commitment?"

"No, of course not. But the unknown superior is not responsible for what happened to him. He told me that if I had informed him, he could have prevented it from happening. I could not trust him enough; that was the problem."

"But who is responsible, then?"

"The other unknown superiors are."

"Anne, what does 'unknown superior' mean? I don't know anything about any of this!"

"Well, this old man belongs to one of the twelve wealthiest families in the world. For hundreds of years, they are the ones who have made all the decisions for which we, the people of little means, have had to pay. I cannot explain everything to you, but it is certain that these people do not necessarily have good intentions for humanity. It is this truth that he wants to reveal. He told them that this book was designed to highlight their good deeds, but just the opposite will be achieved. The book will denounce everything. As long as they weren't aware of that, they could believe that it was just an old man's whim. But they are not stupid, and John's presence with me in Ingolstadt got them thinking since he was a well-known conspiracy believer. I now have evidence that makes me believe that we were followed."

"You know that you are committed to a path that is littered with dangers? If these people are the way you describe them, you don't really measure up to the task, Anne."

"No, there is no risk, neither for me nor for you and Nicolas. As soon as the book is released, they will saturate the market with other titles, denying our statements. But the seed will be sown and people will start thinking. On the other hand, he told me several times that he will not outlive this adventure."

There was a long silence. Anne stood up and came to sit on her husband's knees. "I need to feel that you are with me."

"I know, and I feel hopeless because I am afraid. I would like to tell you, 'Come on! Let's do it! It's a cause worth fighting for.' But I hardly believe it because I have been feeling the danger around us since the beginning and I wonder if it's worth the sacrifice. Nicolas is twelve years old. What will he do if he loses his parents? We have almost no one left! As far as I am concerned, I have the right to give my life! But there is Nicolas, and as a consequence, I lose this right."

"I trust the unknown superior, Hans; he will not allow them to take it out on us. And there is actually no reason for that. The fight is between the twelve families."

"Your superior has got a name?"

"I don't know what his name is. I have a phone number."

Hans sighed, obviously repressing a negative expression. They stood up and hugged each other; their youth and their love did the rest. The next day, Anne took the airplane to Venice with a warm heart.

Chapter 8

The unknown superior welcomed her even more warmly than on the previous occasion. He seemed happy to see her and somewhat worried. "Considering what time it is, my dear, and your desire not to stay late, come and see what was prepared for you."

"I am not very hungry."

"You told me that last time and yet we enjoyed sharing a meal, didn't we?"

"Yes, indeed."

"All right, then. Egg casserole with truffle and fattened chicken salad from Bresse. With that, we shall drink some red Sancerre, which I'm sure you will like."

Anne sat down and couldn't help smiling. "If we had met earlier in another life, I would have proposed a joint venture with you to open a restaurant."

"Have you ever had this idea?"

"Yes, but I don't have the necessary qualifications. And I was dreaming of a very special type of restaurant, extremely expensive to create and manage."

"Tell me more about that."

"Well, first of all, there would be two or three rooms for children. The babies would be looked after by nurses, and the small ones would be supervised by activity organizers, with games and places to rest. The elder ones would be able to watch their cartoons on television. What a pleasure for the parents to have their children near them and yet be able to have a pleasant evening out, don't you think so?"

"It is an excellent idea."

"And then the appetizers would be served in a special lounge, with comfortable armchairs and a light, energetic music. Then the diners would be taken to their tables. Finally, when the meal was finished, the after-dinner drink would be served in another lounge, with deeper armchairs and softer music. But I suppose that I am not the only one to dream of such a place. It certainly exists."

"It certainly does, but far from here. And the hostess may not be as charming as you are. Who knows? Maybe we should think about it again in the near future?"

"My agenda is quite different."

"You are right. Now, tell me, my dear, does your husband remain distant?"

"I have a wonderful husband; he is once again supporting me."

"Ah! You don't know how good it feels to hear that! I know who you are, and therefore I had the conviction that you could never create a family with one of these pretentious lightweights that we so often meet. When life becomes difficult, some people are not as strong as you are. We have equal rights, they say, but we are not equal in our capacities, as can be seen every day."

"I promised him that the Bohemian Club would be my last excursion."

"You did the right thing! I was not intending to impose this last event on you. You are courageous, but the loss of your brother was enough of an ordeal for you. Moreover, after San Francisco, you will know enough to start writing. Having said this, I need some time to neutralize a particularly violent character; I have good reasons to think that he played the main role in the tragedy that you had to endure. That is why I should tell you that you should not give up, Anne! Never give up, not until the book is published and distributed."

"I have given you my word, and you know that. But if my family were to be in danger, I would like you to be honest enough to tell me."

"Nothing will happen to you or to your relatives. Nevertheless, you won't go alone to San Francisco. You will be accompanied by my faithful Young."

"Who is Young?"

"Young is the man who usually drives you from the airport and takes you back. He is like a son to me. He owes me everything, and I owe him everything. We are like two peas in a pod."

"Who are the people that I shall meet over there?"

"Oh! You will be surprised. Only men are accepted. The women attending are generally there because they sell their beauty."

"I am not sure that I would like to be seen as a streetwalker."

"That will not be the case, I can assure you! One need only to look at you! You will also have Young at your side, and you will have your ring. These ladies don't have such rings. You will have an impact on all the participants by your great style, Anne. You are head and shoulders above most of these figures, despite their social status and their bank accounts. And character is what counts the most, don't you think so?"

"Once again, we agree with each other!"

"Another point, Anne: dress casually . These gentlemen of the club enjoy mixing with the riffraff and sometimes indulge in licentious behavior during their yearly meeting in the Bohemian Grove. Also the infrastructure there is rather simple and basic, and I wouldn't want you to catch cold."

He gave her additional information, they agreed on the details of the journey, and they decided that Young would pick her up at home three days later, on Thursday, October 21.

They said their goodbyes, and Anne had the painful feeling that they had just brought an end to their last meeting and that these greetings were a farewell. If she had been rather defensive during their first meeting, the gap had been closed and she now had a feeling for this man that could be called affectionate. She could not remember ever having a relationship so elevated, so intense. The time had come when she should be prepared to see it end. What a pity that was!

She used the next two days to spoil Nicolas and Hans but also to prepare her trip and read her notes. The Bohemian Club, created in 1872 by five journalists, is a very closed neo-conservative club. It has around two thousand members, mostly Americans, with the exception of a few Europeans and, rarely, Asians. The membership fee is twenty-five thousand dollars per year, and the waiting list is a minimum of twenty-one years. Their symbol is an owl, which is burned during the closing session of their gatherings. Many politicians both republican and democrat, artists , entrepreneurs, including people such as Henry Kissinger, George H. W. Bush, and other wealthy individuals. The club is intended to be exclusively a venue for relaxation, where the overworked high and mighty can meet. Once again, it would be important to display signs of recognition. Anne did not forget this.

*

In a splendid office, gently caressed by the last sunbeams of a mild autumn day, Karl, comfortably sitting in a deep armchair, was shaken by a huge laugh. So, then, Bob was afraid for his beautiful girl! The old fool! He was afraid! He would then meet a beautiful end. That would be a triumph!

Chapter 9

Anne took delight in this smooth journey. Young was silent but caring. Taking responsibility for all the logistics, even the most basic, he anticipated her desires. This discrete and elegant man, who had the thin smile of a young monk, and the sharp eyes of a preying bird, was more reassuring than an army of bodyguards. When they arrived in San Francisco, a furious wind had just started. She did not have time to feel chilly: already, a cloak of soft linen had been put on her shoulders. She saw that, of course, as a precaution suggested by the unknown superior, but for Young it seemed to be natural to protect her, even from the wind.

They reached Monte Rio and the Bohemian Grove, a property of 2,700 acres belonging to the club, in the middle of the afternoon on Saturday, October 23, and went to dinner. Young was impressive in his dark suit. Anne was wearing exaggeratedly simple clothes, but she felt it necessary to show her difference from the other women present and so had opted for a long black wool dress with a silk scarf. Her face was bare, and the dress did not have a low neckline. Her only jewels were a string of pearls. She immediately looked so different, just as she had wished, from the women who were there.

Sparkling like Christmas trees, Anne and Young were speaking and laughing loudly. They thus formed a very beautiful couple, and the smiles that they exchanged were interpreted as a clear sign of complicity between a man and a woman which had no ambiguity. They were aware of the confusion and were having fun with it. Young had the easy style of a royal-blooded prince and, though exceedingly discrete, could not hide the pleasure he took in the game. Anne guessed that it was not the first time for him; the unknown superior knew how to use his collaborators and highlight their most subtle talents. They cheered some entertainers performing on stage outdoors. The jazz band was excellent and the meal was abundant though rustic.

Anne was uncomfortable about running into hybrid people with unusual behavior, but once again she came across famous faces, people seen in the press or on television who seemed to be there for fun like any gentleman would do when he is out without his wife. The voices became louder, more bottles were opened. This was considered to be fun in their world! These well-to-do people considered as important men by the people of little means, traveled on private jets, spread out their pot bellies, and urinated on trees, as if marking their territory, something the average working man could never do.

With a simple nod, Young stood up and they left the entertainment to get some rest, agreeing that they would meet again the next morning around ten o'clock. Their accommodations consisted of two different bungalows, and though the place was all right, Anne's sleep was not refreshing.

Young, on the other hand, seemed to be in good shape the next morning. He went to her, holding out his hand. "Did you sleep well?"

"No. And you?"

"I don't believe so."

"You don't believe so?"

"I have to think about it."

Anne smiled. Young's humor was often impenetrable, but she enjoyed it. The wind had fallen and the sunlight was warming the covered terrace, where an enormous breakfast was being served. Young was wearing a velvet suit and Anne, dressed in a white blouse under a very strict gray suit, felt perfectly comfortable in her style as a "different" type of woman. She greeted several people with a hand gesture that offered a favorable view of her ring, all while making the usual signs—the 666 with the left hand and the horned hand with the right hand. Those who came closer to wish her a good appetite were greeted with a Masonic handshake. The smiles confirmed to her that she was recognized.

A fat man, trussed up in a red jacket, leaned a little bit too close to read her badge and started speaking to her while she was trying to enjoy an exquisite omelet with bacon.

"Anne Standfort? I think I know you."

"We met yesterday evening during dinner."

"It was only yesterday evening?"

"I believe so, yes. I am a freelance journalist, and I live in Europe. In fact this is my first visit to the Bohemian Grove. I am preparing a book on behalf of an influential brother."

"Ah, yes? And what is the topic?"

"It is about the truths that should illuminate the world. Do you understand what I mean?"

"Yes, perfectly! Well, once again, enjoy your meal! I shall see you soon?"

"Most probably so."

He did not seem to have understood what kind of illumination Anne was referring to, but he obviously found her charming and only nodded to Young in a very detached manner.

They finished their breakfast and strolled around the park. Always very close, Young remained very reserved, however, and Anne, who would have liked to start a simple and heartfelt conversation, was prevented from doing so. Remarkably delicate, he kept to a very strict relational code, the rules of which apparently had to be scrupulously respected.

Who was this man? Which nation of Asia did he come from? His noble attitude and his exquisite courtesy, which were so fine, were signs of a good background. Or he may have received a special education. In any case, his discrete, protective presence was highly comforting.

*

They attended a debate on climatology that was all but fascinating, and everyone met on the huge, sunny terrace for a glass of champagne. Diverse groups had been formed, and the conversations were lively. When Anne overheard the word *energy* from a group that included a senator and an army officer with many military ribbons on his chest, she left Young and walked closer.

"It seems to me that you are talking about energy, may I join you? Please, gentlemen, keep talking. Energy is my passion!"

"Yes, indeed, the general was giving me the latest news about their project concerning the ZR machine. Have you heard of it?"

"Absolutely not, much to my regret!"

"Officially, it is the most powerful X-ray generator in the world. This machine is located in the main site of Sandia National Laboratories. The most impressive feature of this generator is that it has proved capable of producing temperatures four to six times higher than that of an H-bomb. All these discoveries, coming from the private sector, were made public at the beginning, but we quickly managed to get a grip on things so that today it is classified as top secret! In fact, there are two possible developments. The first in the civil sector is aneutronic fusion, from a boron-hydrogen reaction. A magnetohydrodynamic, or MHD, compressor, derived from the ZR machine, produces a brief impulsive fusion. The energy thus produced during the expansion of the plasma by direct conversion is stored up, for instance, in a simple flywheel, which serves to trigger an alternator."

Anne had not understood one word of this description, as her face certainly expressed. The general continued, "In plain language, my friend, this technology facilitates a simple production of electricity from very abundant combustibles, such as hydrogen and boron. This power station would not yield any waste since the product of this reaction is helium, the gas used to inflate children's balloons in fairs. It is revolutionary, but these power stations will never be in service, which is good news for my friends the oil magnates! For us, there is a much more interesting application: a clean bomb!"

"This is extraordinary! What progress!" Anne, proving herself to be quite the actress, skillfully displayed her admiration.

"You can say that again! As you know, the detonator of a fusion bomb is a fission bomb, but it is impossible to miniaturize it because of the famous critical mass. Above all, it is terribly polluting. It cannot easily be used because the irradiated dust, carried by the wind, is likely to fall on our own troops. But with this miraculous technology, the same MHD compressor, derived from a miniature Z machine, could serve as an H-bomb detonator thanks to the fabulous energy that it yields. The same fusion as in the civil case would produce a nonpolluting bomb. You can imagine the applications on the battlefield! The research is progressing well, and we should soon reap the fruit of our efforts."

"We at last have a radical, and hopefully final, solution to this soaring demography! We shall get rid of all these useless larvae we must currently put up with!"

"Absolutely! I like to hear you say it so clearly! You might like to know that this is not the only area where the military-industrial complex is working to support our ultimate goal. They are also at the cutting edge in the fields of climatic weapons—thanks to HAARP—bacteriological weapons, and seismic weapons."

"Seismic weapons?"

"Yes! There too we have achieved much progress. We have mastered the compact machines and the intense but very short energy bursts produced by an MHD. Unfortunately we have not yet managed to trigger an earthquake where and when we choose, but we are conducting numerous experiments in seismic areas."

"This, then, is the reason why there have been so many earthquakes lately? Bravo! It's good to know that such progress is being made. We are fortunate to have people like you who take seriously the future of our planet. Well, I am delighted to have got to know you and I hope to see you soon!"

Anne, feeling totally disgusted, went back to Young. "Young, if it is all right with you, I would like you to accompany me. I need to breathe some fresh air."

Without answering, he offered his arm and they went deep under the trees into the heart of the forest. They walked, not speaking but simply enjoying the sound of the birds singing and of the wind blowing through the leaves.

When they came back to the center of activities, it was close to four o'clock. The show was at its peak, and a second band was playing loudly. They headed for the bar where, since morning, an excellent French champagne had been freely flowing.

Anne sat in an armchair, glass in her hand, hoping to find a moment of rest despite the noisy atmosphere. Her hope was short-lived; her ring was conspicuous and had undoubtedly attracted the sticky man with a hypocritical smile who had begun talking to her. This place definitely offered many opportunities for making contacts, as the old man had informed her, and she was forced to play the game.

The man was as talkative as he was overweight. He sat down beside her, unconcerned about being far too close for comfort, and started the conversation. Very quickly, there was a change of topic. Anne, willing to learn as much as possible, had opened the way for him, saying that she had little contact with the 'brethren' in America, and that religious practices in Europe were more restricted. She was not prepared, however, to hear what the man, obviously comfortable with this issue, was about to reveal.

"Yes, you are absolutely right. Religious practices are remarkably organized in the United States. We serve and honor Lucifer, the good God, as it should be. I take the opportunity of this gathering of the Bohemian Club, with its grand finale, to recruit well-to-do people. This is the right place for doing so. As I speak to you, I am working as an active member of a pedophile network. The members belong to the middle and higher classes. We meet regularly during these secret ceremonies, which you are certainly familiar with. By the way, the media world is an excellent resource. Take many pop singers, for example, who uses many occult signs in their videos. Many of them are actively using subliminal messages to prepare people's minds for Lucifer's coming reign."

Anne, throughout this speech, had imperceptibly tilted her champagne glass. At the end of this last sentence, she improvised a superb sneeze that, as a result, spilled the icy liquid on the man's trousers. She had not done it on purpose, but the wet place proved to be very strategic. It was hard for her to hold back an irrepressible desire to laugh while offering her most sincere apologies. The sensation must have been unpleasant, and totally ignoring her apologies, he ran out and disappeared.

Anne was heading to the bar to refill her glass with champagne when she met Young, who was coming from the opposite side. No one, fortunately, noticed the look they gave each other, which expressed a total repulsion toward this group of people.

A little later, she overheard a conversation between a man who introduced himself as a university professor and other political leaders, including one whose face was already familiar to her, though she could not remember his name. The topic, once again, was far from being insignificant. They were discussing man's responsibility in climate change; the professor was arguing that man's responsibility was largely exaggerated. He was expressing various points, one of which particularly struck Anne. According to him, during the historical periods of global warming, the increase of carbon dioxide had always appeared after a temperature increase. In other words, it was not carbon dioxide that had caused warming, but the opposite. What's more, he added, the warming in question was mostly caused by a more intense activity of the sun, and human production had only a small influence. The real danger could more likely come from a solar eruption of great magnitude, which would be accompanied by radiation able to destroy a fair number of electronic components in computers and other communication systems that are not protected. This would cause an apocalyptic chaos.

Anne took the opportunity to say something. "Yet I have heard from a reliable source that the climatologic models are well conceived and based on reliable data."

"Dear friend, were you ever told that you were a bit naive?"

"Yes, indeed, but I saw that as a compliment for my being young." Anne, playing a true character part, was simpering the best she could.

"No doubt, no doubt. But you must know, my dear young friend, that these models are based on so many hypothesis. The historical data you see as reliable are adjusted to produce results showing the influence of human activity in this warming. However, as far as I am concerned, as long as my department confirms this reality, I shall remain a well-known expert and most of all money will keep flowing. And even if, in the scientific community, there are many who question the official thesis, those skeptics have no access to the media. The main thing is that the general public remains convinced of the mortal danger represented by carbon dioxide, and this will allow for the establishment of a carbon emission market. The financial impact is astronomical, and the banks are already watering at the mouth at the idea of the profits they will make. Besides, it maintains a climate of fear that is favorable to the development of an ideology based on the Gaia theory. I am not telling you anything you don't already know if I say that humanity cannot continue its exponential growth while our resources are limited. In order to solve this problem, we just have to claim that the earth will have to react to the activity of such a quantity of useless microbes and preserve itself. This can be achieved only by inducing a fever; climate change itself will cause floods, followed by extreme drought. Thus harvests will be destroyed and there will be starvation. At the same time, we will advise all that the earth is also triggering earthquakes and causing diseases. Our ultimate goal will at last be reached through a drastic population decrease."

The group was unanimously approving. It would have been useless to try to find a contradictory opinion. Anne, feeling she had heard enough, excused herself and left. She joined another group and decided it would be the last. She was reaching the limits of what her nerves could endure.

This group was talking about food processing and pharmaceutical products. There were many congratulations for having managed, through some politicians in complete support of "the cause," to slip in the recent laws reforming health care in the United States a provision allowing the subcutaneous implantation of an electronic microchip smaller than a grain of rice in each citizen. It would contain only medical information in the initial stage but would later include other types of information, so that every movement of anyone carrying such a chip could be followed.

Anne launched once again a simple question regarding the regeneration of the species. The question was immediately welcomed enthusiastically by a representative of a pharmaceutical firm, who boasted of having introduced a component based on mercury and aluminium, which has a harmful impact on health, into vaccinations. However, the population had been reassured through a massive effort of studies and conclusions proving the opposite.

The conversation then drifted to another topic, the urgent need to eliminate small family farms through the imposition of norms that would be impossible to respect. This elimination would pave the way for mass production. Costs would be reduced and quality was unimportant. Genetically modified organisms offered negligible benefits since they contained in their genes the pesticides which would protect them. Of course, research done on animals had proved that these products were toxic, but these studies, once conducted, could easily be stifled. That was part of the game.

Anne was exhausted. She would have given anything to be able to leave the place, but she had to attend the final ceremony, which did not start until eleven o'clock that night. Before that, she would have to get through dinner. No doubt, the conversations in the evening would be far less informative; these gentlemen, after drinking so much champagne and having their minds misted with the heady fumes of alcohol, would have much more down-to-earth concerns. Already she had perceived some glances that said a lot about these men's desires. Anne knew that she was pretty and desirable, but she did not feel flattered at all by the indiscrete attentions directed at her. Each time, she would ostensibly turn her head away. Discouraged, she decided to move closer to Young, who understood the move and offered his arm. She still had to sit through some shows and laugh at the humor of some entertainers. Feeling fed up, she had the feeling that she was wasting time and the only thing that mattered was the dial of her watch, which moved ever so slowly. Young managed to look as stoic as a Roman emperor.

Finally it was dinnertime, but even that was hell. The fat man with the red jacket, ignoring Young once again, had hurried to sit near her, and was fawning over her with shallow politeness. Coming close to a nervous breakdown, she was unable to swallow anything, and the fat man insisted that she taste every dish, even holding a spoon as if trying to feed her. He himself was gulping huge mouthfuls, and just seeing this was enough to cut her appetite.

At the very moment when she thought that she would have to become unpleasant and stand up to go somewhere else, Young anticipated her need and helped her leave. They walked away, watched by the flabbergasted eyes of the big man.

"Thank you, Young, I was about to explode!"

"Yes, I noticed."

"Not too much, I hope?"

"Even a blind man would have seen it."

Again, the humor of Young made Anne smile. He had the right words and could describe the situation with a hilarious simplicity. There was nothing else to be added. They continued walking. It was 10:30. They could quietly head to the ceremony site. When this was over, they would be able to leave. The mission would be accomplished and the punishment would be over.

They were among the first to take a seat and were placed so that they had a panoramic view of the stage. Night had fallen, and the lights of thousands of candles created an eerie atmosphere as the "festivities" had not even started. The unknown superior had briefed Anne about the sequence of events. Feeling a numb apprehension, her heart beat quickly.

A kind of lake separated the spectators from the stage, where important figures were standing, similar to druids, dressed in long white robes. They were surrounding a mossy boulder covered with straw, the shape of which imitated a huge owl about thirty feet high. Below that, Anne could distinguish something that looked like an altar.

As eleven o'clock approached, a steady stream of people arrived. All the participants found their seats and the music started. At last the speaker began shouting endless injunctions and professions of faith in a loud voice.

Anne was getting numb with the cold. She suddenly noticed a boat that was slowly moving on the water and at last reached the bottom of the stage. A kind of shroud that was small in size, as for a child, was carried to the altar by the men in white robes.

The music intensified into a crescendo. Even though Anne knew that all of this was only a sham, she could feel her heart pounding.

In the following second, flames came to life at the foot of the owl and the whole thing flared up like a torch as a booming voice, which seemed to come out of the statue, screamed, "You are now burning me, but I shall be reborn. Next year, I shall be back."

The show was gruesome, and Anne could not but wonder how so many important people, many claiming to be good Christians, could take part in it.

Officially, the incineration symbolized the elimination of worries and problems for the members of the club. But the old unknown superior had revealed to her a deeper meaning. The statue represented Moloch, a God to whom the Ammonites, a Canaanite tribe, would sacrifice their firstborn children by throwing them in the fire. And following these ideas, he had explained to her that in the Kabalist tradition, which had led to Palladism, Lucifer was not a cursed angel but an angel who gives light and regenerates when he is burnt. It is always the same old myth of the God who dies. Anne thought of her son and became afraid. Was he really protected?

There was a loud round of applause. Young, with authority, took her arm. They left as if they were escaping. Their car was waiting in the car park.

*

Since she had come back from the United States, Anne had been living at her desk, working twelve hours a day. She had first made a precise outline. Anyone should be able to understand this book, which should be convincing and based on a verifiable chronology. Any person willing to think more deeply should be able to reconstruct the whole picture through articles or situations reported by the media. The task was arduous. There was a risk that the reader might feel confused if things were traced very far back in the past. The report would lose its credibility if it failed to mention the beginnings of debt money. It was indeed a report. She really felt that she had received a mission to report on a serious situation for humanity.

She had spent a whole night explaining everything revealed by the unknown superior to Hans, who had been dumbfounded. Then he had read the notes that she had taken and, in the chilly morning, while drinking his coffee, had told Anne that he felt stained and was contemplating looking for another job.

Life returned to normal for a few days...until Thursday, October 28.

Chapter 10

On Thursdays Nicolas went to the gym after leaving school. He would thus come home an hour later, around five o'clock. Night was already falling when Anne looked at her watch. It was five thirty. Nicolas had not come home. She thought that Hans had gone to pick him up, and a few minutes later she called on his mobile phone.

"Hans, is Nicolas with you?"

"No, I am still in the office. I shall finish in five minutes."

"But he is not back yet!"

"Today is Thursday. He goes to the gym"

"Yes, but he is usually back at five and it is already five thirty."

"He probably went to see his friend David."

After hanging up, Anne called David's parents. They had not seen Nicolas. When Anne ended the call, she started to panic. Nicolas was never late. She called Hans again.

"David has not seen Nicolas."

"I am going to the gym right now."

Anne stayed at the window until Hans came home.

When he arrived, out of breath, he shouted from the entrance, "Anne, Nicolas did not go to the gym today!"

"What?"

"I met the coach. He was leaving the hall when I arrived."

"But where did he go?"

Anne's whole body was shaking. Like a robot, she went and picked up her phone and dialed a telephone number. Someone answered, and in front of Hans, who was dumfounded, she screamed in the phone as if she were mad. "They took my son! They took my son! They took my son! You swore that they would not do us any harm! They took Nicolas!"

Hans took the telephone from her hands as she burst into tears.

"I am Hans, Nicolas's father! Where is he?"

"I know who you are, Hans. Listen to me!"

"I don't want to listen to you! I want my son!"

"Hans, be quiet; you must listen to me. No harm will be done to your son, I promise! And your son is a remarkable little boy! But you will have to do as I say. Prepare luggage for both of you for about eight days. I know what is going on, and I shall explain it to you as soon as we meet. For the time being, a private jet will be reserved for you. Young, my collaborator, will pick you up on Sunday afternoon. Anne knows him; you will be safe with him."

"I can't believe you. I am calling the police!"

"Hans, think. Anne has explained everything to you. You should know that this is not the solution. If you trust me, on Sunday, at the latest, you will hold your son in your arms and he will be safe."

"Why Sunday?"

"We shall go to Jerusalem. They will take Nicolas there. I will explain everything to you. For the moment, take care of Anne, I beg you. There are people who want her to attend a ceremony, though I had told her that she did not need to be there. The three of us will go there, and you will be reunited with Nicolas. Once again, please trust me. Do you have any sedatives among your medicines?"

"I think so."

"Take a pill and make sure that Anne does the same. You have to remain calm until Sunday."

"All right."

"I am on your side, Hans. They are trying to intimidate you, nothing else. Things will be all right, I promise you."

"I suppose that I have no other option than to lay my son's life in your hands."

"You won't regret it. See you soon."

Anne was crying convulsively in an armchair. "I beg you to forgive me, Hans."

"My darling, guilt is useless. Let us gather our strength to face this ordeal. The two of us—I hope three or four of us—will face this together."

"Three or four?"

"The voice of your old man reassured me. You told me that he was very powerful and that his assistant, this Young, was reliable. Do you still believe it?"

"Yes, they did nothing wrong. The problem is all the others. The book is disturbing them."

"Then we must follow his instructions, prepare ourselves to leave, and remain calm. Nicolas should not return to a devastated family."

Anne and Hans spent two days in a state of shock, without going out, feeling like animals trapped in a cage. At last, on Sunday, October 31, at one o'clock in the afternoon the limousine of the unknown superior was waiting for them at the gate of their building. Young shook Han's hand, took their travel bags, opened the door for them, and said, "Don't worry. The jet is waiting for you at the airport. Everything will be all right."

Chapter 11

Bob could not keep from calling Karl.

"Dear friend, I have just learned that you have kidnapped the child. Was that really necessary?"

"Without any doubt, my friend. You claim that your journalist will be perfectly educated without attending one of our ceremonies? And surely the most important ceremony is the Luciferian New Year. How can we be sure that her story will be authentic?"

"The book will be released only after I have carefully read it."

"All right, all right, but without any intention to sound unpleasant, we are not immortal, my friend, and your great age is not protecting you from a problem. Imagine that you were no longer here to guarantee a serious proofreading?"

"You would do a perfect job instead of me, I am sure. In any case, I consider that the anxiety caused to the journalist is not a good thing for my project. It is my last gift, I remind you."

"Come on, let's not look at the negative side of things. She will be reunited with her child over there! And then she will be able to witness the power of our organization vividly. Your book will sound even more accurate."

"All right. I count on you that the child will not to be harmed in any way."

"Do you take me to be a torturer?"

"I suggest that we conclude this conversation on October 31. For the moment, I think that we have talked about the essential points."

Bob was sweating when he hung up. This verbal joust had exhausted him. He had the awful sensation of having displayed his anxiety and of having shown his weakness. No doubt that Karl had deeply enjoyed their exchange and would take advantage of any perceived fear.

*

Bob—who had traveled from the United States to Jerusalem, the spiritual center of the great monotheist religions—had been in the city for a few hours and had arrived at the immense property where the temple had been built. His family had largely contributed to this project, as well as to the establishment of the State of Israel, all done in a discrete and efficient way. Most families were upset to see what the Zionist and Palestinian extremists had done with this investment. But this was now the least of his concerns.

A huge park surrounded the temple, its fifty columns, and its monumental steps. Externally, the majestic building, about sixty feet high, with its imposing statues, was the exact copy of the great altar of Pergamon, an ancient city in what is now Turkey. Saint John called this temple the throne of Satan. It was used to sacrifice animals and later Christians, and it had been dedicated to Zeus.

Bob had come there on many occasions, but never in such a mood. Today, his anxiety was great. With much lucidity, he analyzed his feeling of complete hopelessness. As far as he was concerned, the term *hopeless* was now taking its full meaning. Hope had indeed vanished, and his path on this earth would end in a few hours. Karl would not pass up the opportunity to boast in front of Lucifer in the most arrogant way. He would not spare him. Actually, Bob had not even thought about escaping. The main thing had been gained; his gift to mankind would be delivered.

When Anne was safe, the book would be released. She would not fail. This woman had brought him more truth in a few weeks than his relatives had during the last thirty years. He did not feel any bitterness, however, knowing that he was responsible for this situation, and in this moment, he wished fervently that his children would not be like him or mourn him and that their projects in life would be the opposite of what his had been.

On October 31, 2010, he had only one duty to complete: Anne, Hans, and Nicolas had to outlive this nightmare. They would not be unscathed—he was aware of that—but they must stay alive. He had said his farewell to Young, whose emotion had been visible under his reserve. Everything was organized; Young would be the one to take care of the three of them. He would take them out of the temple and would hide them long enough that their security could be absolutely guaranteed.

An immense nostalgia kept lingering in Bob's heart: he had not had time to offer more kindness to this outstanding lady. He had given her money, much money, and she did not know what to do with it. She still saw it as dirty money, which could be purified only if it was used for humanitarian work. She would not keep anything. And he—who at the very end of his journey on this earth, had met a beautiful soul, able to give without asking anything except the conviction of having done something useful for the sake of others—had found nothing but money to give her! What a pity! He had certainly met such people, but he had not recognized them. This thought was now torturing him and justified his disappearance.

At this moment, Young called him and announced that Anne and Hans had just landed. He climbed up the steps and waited in the entrance. Above him, the code of conduct of the rosy cross was engraved—"Intus ut libet, foris ut moris est," meaning "In private think what you wish, in public behave as is the custom." In other words, "we may cheat our contemporaries, claiming to agree with the current ideas, but secretly, let us think and act as we wish." In fact, he knew it now, this motto was particularly relevant for the master of the house, the greatest hoaxer—Lucifer himself. Anne would most probably notice it, and she had to leave the place alive in order to bear witness. She was so pale that it worried him; she also seemed to have lost much weight.

Hans approached him rapidly, obviously trying to control his anger. "Where is Nicolas?"

"Don't worry. I know that he is all right."

"Yes, but have you seen him?"

"Not yet."

"Then how can you be so sure?"

"I know it! It would be in nobody's interest to do any harm to your son. You will attend the ceremony, and then Young will take the three of you far from here. Come in. I shall take you to the hall before things get started."

Anne had not yet uttered a word. Her big blue eyes were staring at him with an overwhelming power, and her eyes cried out with the desperate trust that she placed in him at this moment. Young was standing beside her as if he expected at any moment to have to catch her.

Hans was pacing back and forth, like a furious ox. "You will follow my instructions. I am Nicolas's father. I want to see him immediately and keep him with me and his mother. I hope that you clearly understand what I said! If you don't comply, things will not end well for you!"

"Hans! There is no point in threatening me. I did not play any role in Nicolas's kidnapping. To try to convince you is pointless, I know. Yet I have the obligation to convince you that the three of us are to attend this ceremony and—more than that—we have to play the game. Under that condition, you will see your son and will be able to leave this place. I ask you to believe me. I know these people. I was part of their world for almost all of my life. I know their rules."

"You have dragged my wife into this appalling farce with no scruples!"

"Once again, Hans, if I could have imagined what was going to happen, I would never have contacted your wife. Having said this, she is a pure jewel. Her soul is beautiful, and she has understood the essential role that she could play for the sake of all humanity. Model your attitude on hers, please!"

Bob led them into a room, which was small and without windows; the furniture consisted of a table and four chairs. On the table, there was a tray and three glasses. Bob then explained what these glasses, filled with a strange liquid, were. They would have to drink this liquid in order to be able to attend the ceremony and meet their son. To prove that the beverage was not poisoned, he suggested that each of them choose their glass. He would take the last glass and drink before them.

Anne showed no reaction, but when Hans refused adamantly, Bob gave them a more precise explanation. "We have five physical senses, which enable our physical body to interact with the physical world, and we have five spiritual senses, which enable us to taste, see, smell, hear, and touch what exists in the spirit world. This world is a parallel world where our spiritual body continues to live after our physical death. Each person possesses this spiritual body, but for some reasons, and with the exception of some mediums, our spiritual senses are—how should I put it—anesthetized. The spirit world seems to be nonexistent since we have no way to perceive it. The beverage is in these glasses, the composition of which traces back to antiquity, enables a provisional opening of these five spiritual senses. Don't worry. Unlike with a drug, you will keep your reason and your faculties."

Hans exploded. "You take me for a fool, but you are mistaken. Keep your hallucinogenic charlatanism and take me to my son!"

Anne seemed to wake up. "Hans, remember that we decided to come here and do what was necessary to find Nicolas, at any cost. I am convinced that there is no danger."

She took a glass and swallowed the contents in one gulp. Bob invited Hans to take his glass. He complied, and Bob drank from the remaining glass.

"Now, rest for a moment. I shall come back for you a few moments before the ceremony starts."

Anne came closer to the unknown superior, asking him a silent question, which he understood immediately.

"No, Anne, it is not a ceremony in front of the God who dies. What's more, as soon as it is over, you will be under the protection of Young." With his two hands, he strongly grasped the young woman's shoulders and then went out, locking the door behind him.

*

For Karl, this date of October 31, 2010, would be a landmark. It would at last bring him the consecration he had been waiting for. This October 31 would seal his personal triumph in front of the other families. He would reveal Bob's betrayal and be the main actor of his fall in front of the master himself. And then, in order to complete his work, he would offer him the content of the vial. He had what he considered a brilliant idea; it was important that he could get all possible advantages from it. Nothing could be more normal. Then he would be chosen as the elected one. There was no doubt about that.

He entered the triangular room, the Sanctum Regnum, inhaled the air, and meditated in front of the setting, always so impressive. The armchair reserved for Bob, where he would sit for the last time, elicited a sharp smile on Karl's face.

He gazed at the throne, where the master would sit, and the statue of stone representing the Templar Baphomet, which the Palladists call the "palladium" and for which he had a strong attachment. Is not a symbol the visible image of an invisible reality? He contemplated it for a long time. It was the Ark of the Covenant between Lucifer and mankind, just as the Ark of the Covenant of Moses symbolized the covenant between God and his chosen people. God spoke from between the two cherubim. On the Baphomet, the horns replaced the two cherubim of the biblical ark, and Lucifer would appear through a bluish flame located between the two horns. There was something magic there, and Karl had always been sensitive to it.

At the foot of the statue there was a skull that, according to legend, was that of Jacques de Molay, the last Templar master who died on the stake, and last conservator of the antique statue before the twelve families.

The statue was about three feet high. With its wings in the back, and its great horns, it had an appearance that was both frightening and fragile, set as it was on the red tablecloth that covered the altar.

Karl's gaze moved over these impressive surroundings, which he saw as being his. The great hall, with its high walls of black granite and its floor in black and white squares, had a very particular shape. The triangle was everywhere. The room was triangular; the altar was triangular and placed intentionally like a shining eye at the extreme edge of the shape. Heavy doors of precious wood were set in the walls. The paintings, the brocade curtains on the walls—everything spoke to him of the glory of his master, Lucifer, and he was satisfied and happy. He was also impatient. He prepared the sacrificial knife. Later on, the knife would be used to offer three adults and a child to the master. The guards were ready to offer their support when the time came. He put the Korean vial at the foot of the statue and lit ten candles displayed on a satanic pentagram, having the statue at its center. Exactly 120 days had passed since the time when the worshippers of Adonai had been sacrificed, and Karl felt a burning impatience to substantiate his offering.

*

Everything was unfolding perfectly, but neither Karl nor Bob could imagine what would take place in front of their eyes. At this hour, they knew nothing of a plan devised at another level and emanating from a will far higher than theirs.

*

When Anne entered the room, she had completely recovered and was strong. Whether it was caused by the beverage, she could not say. It seemed to her, however, that her overall vision had been sharpened tenfold. She thus immediately noticed the knife, and her eyes met Bob's for a fraction of a second, allowing her to see the anxiety in them. All her muscles became stiff, and she felt both ready and invincible. None of the actors in this devilish room would prevent her from saving her son. She straightened her shoulders, feeling confident in her resources.

 The other families, in other words the Luciferian clergy, had already taken their seats and were chanting in Latin. Anne recognized a formula that she had come across during her research: "Dei optimi maximi ad gloriam," or "To the glory of God, the best and the greatest." She understood that it referred to Lucifer.

 Bob came and sat on the seat closest to the altar, showing his position in the hierarchy. Hans and Anne were invited to move to his left. No seats had been prepared for them, so they had to stand, as if they were being sentenced.

 Hans took his wife's hand in his and was surprised to feel that it was firm and strong, like a stone, whereas his own hand was irrepressibly shaking.

 Karl, standing slightly back, examined the trio with self-importance.

Just at the moment when the room, which thus far had been quite dim, lit up and as the doors were about to close, a guard came in with Nicolas. He was wearing light clothes and sandals and walked very straight, looking intently in front of him. Hans opened his arms. Anne was sobbing and screaming at the same time. The child ran to his parents, who surrounded him tightly.

From that moment, Anne had a strange sensation, as if reality had entered another dimension. She looked at Hans: he was clasping Nicolas but was still shaking. His bulging eyes expressed panic. Turning her head toward the unknown superior, she met his eyes and received the message to remain calm and everything would be all right. Her power and determination had returned. Their salvation consisted, without any possible doubt, in the capacity to watch what was going on as observers and not as participants. She received from this man, who was facing death with serenity, a great lesson of courage; she would not disappoint him.

She feared, however, that Hans could not take this much longer. Unhesitatingly, she took his arm and held it tight. With her right hand, she brought Nicolas closer, propping him against her, and she looked at both with a peaceful smile.

Suddenly the surroundings took on another appearance. The floor was covered with greenish sparks the size of a pin, yet they did not produce any warmth. The statue and its frightening mask were illuminated. Then the sparks grew also on the walls, from the bottom to the top. When they reached the ceiling, Anne thought that the beverage had fulfilled its role. She now had to be focused and in control of her thoughts in order not to weaken and to remain conscious. Her role as a human being, in this place, at this time, was essential and was beyond anything she could have imagined. She felt that she was responsible to complete this mission alone. The man who shared her life and who was the father of her child had great and beautiful qualities. Yet she could not expect a reaction from him adapted to this kind of situation. In a fraction of a second, she thought that she could expect a greater serenity from Nicolas. But the main thing was for her to keep the appropriate attitude. There was no more time to feel guilt or to shed tears. She had some degree of responsibility in the death of John; Hans and Nicolas had to get out of this awful adventure with a minimum of after-effects. She breathed deeply several times; these thoughts had brought strength to her.

Then there were the knocks. First there were three quick knocks, like thunderbolts. Then there was only one knock and then two of an extreme violence. Hans started. Nicolas was stiff. The statue seemed to vanish, and a seventh knock was heard, even more violent. The appearance of the throne had changed, it was now covered with gold.

Anne mentally clutched each of her muscles in order to remain conscious. Her brain had to remain active and her senses awakened. She had to "see" in order to be able to translate what she was seeing into words, words which she would be able to write, words that would be read, words that would inform humanity.

The character, still blurred but taking shape in a myriad of golden lights, was dressed with a kind of shimmering mail coat and seemed to have a fascinating beauty. Was this Lucifer? But he seemed to be truly made of flesh and bones! If that was the case, one had to agree that the special effects were well done! But how many tricks, how many lighting effects were necessary to look credible and be respected!

Anne was now completely relaxed. Feeling proud of herself and her strength, she thought that she would not buy into all this and that she would indeed be the faithful reporter that Bob expected. He had not lied, and the figure that was there in front of her in all its splendor was undoubtedly able to hoodwink people, including he who would lose his life today.

And then he talked, and the voice that came out of this throat sounded like what one would expect—egocentric, falsely deep, deliberately enticing. "My dear children! I am so happy to meet you for this New Year! You know that we have little time left to set up the great revolution and liberate mankind from the evil grip of Adonai."

Anne remembered what Bob had told her: Adonai is what Lucifer calls God.

"For generations, I have chosen you and I have showered rewards upon you so that you would answer my call. But I am disappointed! Your own children are not as motivated as you were, and you are no longer as united as before. I have made such an effort to help you. I have a hard life. I have only one goal, to liberate you! And what do you offer to me in return? Very few things, in reality! You, my little Robert, I worry very much about you, you who are the first. Three months have gone by and you have not invoked me even one time! You know that I can do nothing if you don't invite me. You were absent during my last ceremony, and today you come before me with this family. I see a sacrificial knife prepared on the altar. Do you intend to sacrifice them to be forgiven?"

Karl made a step forward, opening his mouth to say something. Lucifer raised his hand with violence. Karl moved back quickly and sat down.

Bob declared, "I have invited Anne Standfort in order to introduce her to you. I asked her—and this is my gift—to write a book that will talk about you to the world."

Lucifer examined Anne for a long time, not without rebuking Karl, who was apparently trying to say something again. "You remind me of a woman with whom I was intimate a long time ago. A book about me? Why not? It is time to correct the injustice directed against me, which makes me suffer so much. But I feel that you are tense. Are you afraid of me? I don't want to harm you in any way. I am merciless with my enemies, yet I am exceedingly caring for my children. Ask the families attending here. They will tell you that I have greatly rewarded them for generations. Each time they turn to me, I bring them good luck and fulfill all their desires, above all the most shameful..." He had a coarse throat laugh. "But whoever is not with me is against me! Which camp will you choose, Anne?"

"That of the truth."

"Ah! The truth...the truth is that I am tired of all these sacrifices offered to me. I expect something else from my children! Alas, because of Adonai, men are stagnating in ignorance. In 2001, just before the attacks I inspired so brilliantly my disciples in England offered me a holocaust of five hundred thousand animals in order to please me but also so that I would bless these attacks. You did not know that, Anne? Think back! These animals had foot-and-mouth disease. This sickness is contagious but rarely mortal. But the animals were all sacrificed just like in Babylonian times! Not only this, but on December 24, 2009, other disciples in the Netherlands offered forty thousand sheep and goats. These animals were supposed to have the Q fever. Between us, I liked the date chosen, the birthday of the bastard!"

Anne remembered having heard about the massive slaughter of flocks. She was now completely quiet. Hans was not moving. She could feel Nicolas breathing peacefully, tightly holding her. Everything was going as expected. The fear had left her, and minute by minute she was recording with an intense concentration all the elements that would feed her book.

When Lucifer was about to continue, Karl made another attempt. Lucifer interrupted him sharply. "Have I ever allowed you to interrupt me? Is this a new form of arrogance? I suggest that you control yourself. This ceremony is guided by me and me alone!"

Karl withdrew into the shadows.

"As I was just saying, the choice of the date of Christmas moved me. Quite often, small human babies, even infants, are sacrificed to please me, but in truth, Anne, it is Adonai who puts trouble in the mind of those who want to follow me, even if I am not indifferent to this testimony of worship. It is an impressive offering, but in the end, it doesn't matter to me if animals or babies created by Adonai are offered to me. Therefore, don't worry. If you are my friend, no one will sacrifice you in front of me this evening. Adonai has spread the idea that I am the one who inspires fear in the heart of man. It is a lie and an unfair attack! Anne, are you afraid of me?"

"No!"

"You want to proclaim the truth in a book? I am going to tell you what this truth is all about. Adonai created the world. Then he created men to make slaves of them; blinded by superstition, they worship him without trying to understand since he keeps them in ignorance. Well, I ask you, what on earth is greater than reason and knowledge? When I understood his goal, I rebelled and, ever since that time, have continued trying to liberate man from the yoke of Adonai. Man is reduced to the status of a barbarian animal! I am fighting to share my knowledge with him and elevate him to my divine light. I have adopted mankind, making it my family. You are my offspring. This is the truth, and it is very simple. Do you understand me?"

"Yes, I do."

"You say yes but I don't feel that you are convinced. That is normal. Adonai has distorted your spirit with his false truths. I see on your finger a ring that bears the Palladian symbol of Noah's dove, which reminds me of an early example. Though it was long ago and human beings were not numerous, Adonai did not hesitate one second to drown them. Why? They had liberated themselves and refused to worship him. They wanted to be free in their thoughts and their deeds, but Adonai is cruel. They learned that at their expense. Read the Bible again, Anne, and you will see the number of massacres of innocents that he has demanded. His 'chosen people' became an exterminating people. How many of my poor children have they murdered? Today, again, see all these people killed on behalf of Allah! Who starts wars? Who generates the sicknesses and the starvation? Adonai, as he has always done. Adonai, who, no matter what, will not raise a finger to prevent disasters. He rejoices to see the suffering of mankind. It pains me. But now I have a precise question to ask you, Anne. How many holy wars have there been in my name? How many? Not one, you will agree. Then, I am asking you, who is the good God, he or me? Do you understand why I am talking about an injustice? Is it normal?"

"No, it isn't."

"It puts me in a state of revolt. Forgive me if you perceive anger in my voice, but I hate injustice. Have you ever seen Adonai, Anne?"

"No, I haven't."

"You see, this is the evidence that he is hiding. But unlike him, I am a God who does not fear to show himself, and I appear to those who truly desire to see me. What about you, Anne. Do you desire me?"

The question was expressed in a strange way, and Anne was speechless. Suddenly, she felt that Nicolas was straightening and was moving away from her. With purpose and poised, he moved, his posture invigorated by a mission, strong in his belief!

He made two steps toward the altar, and from his throat, an unknown voice came out, stronger than his child's voice and more guttural. "Is it not God who originally created you as an angel? Is it not against your creator that you revolted? And is it not your rebellion that has brought chaos and introduced evil in the divine creation?"

The audience was stirred and shocked by the impertinent child. Karl made a new attempt but was rebuked by Lucifer. "I don't need anyone to answer a child's question, Karl, especially you!"

Hans made a movement to pull Nicolas back. Anne was also worried, but she kept Hans from doing it. Nicolas's eyes were abnormal, rolled upward, and she thought that what was going on now, however incomprehensible, certainly had some reason. Again, she met Bob's eyes, which comforted her. She had no choice but to trust her son.

Lucifer continued with a sweet voice. "Little immature man, you are mistaken! You see, I don't have wings in my back. It is Adonai who perpetuates this false truth. Fortunately, I am here to put you back on the right track."

Nicolas made another small step forward. His voice had changed slightly and sounded even more confident. "It must have been an ordeal for you to see God give birth to human beings, his sons and daughters of flesh and blood, whereas you don't even have a physical body and will never be able to create a family like mine, for instance. Then you saw God love this emerging humanity, and you suffered when you thought that he loved them more than you and would treat them differently from you. This is where you made a mistake. God did not stop loving you. You were his favorite angel, his masterpiece before the creation of the physical world. He granted you all his knowledge. You were as splendid as the false image that you are now giving. But you did not understand anything. And now you protest against injustice. Is it really unjust?"

"I am enduring the greatest injustice. Who are you to imagine what is going on in my head and attribute thoughts to me?"

"What is going on in your head is not difficult to understand. And as I am a child, I shall give you a simplified image. Imagine a master who creates a great empire with a faithful and very intelligent servant. This servant, convinced he is to one day inheriting all of the empire, serves his master joyfully for many years. But one day the master and his wife have children, and the servant understands that master's love for his children is far greater than his love for the servant. The servant realizes that the inheritance will not be for him. He sees himself trapped in the role of a servant—to the master, first of all, and then to his children. An immense jealousy mounts in him, and he thinks, 'Ah! You think that your children are higher than me? Well, I shall drag them down in decadence, and you will see which of the two will remain noble and pure.' This is your story; you are a traitor who has dragged the people down so that they become merciless and commit atrocities, which allows you to tell God today that his children are worse than you! It is very simple—you are jealous!"

"Jealous? Me? Jealous of what? Of a primitive humanity consisting of ignorant beings worse than animals? How could I ever feel any trace of jealousy in front of such inferiority?"

The voice of Lucifer was twisted by hatred. One could almost hear him groan. A child was standing firm in front of him! He had the power to immediately stop this masquerade, which ridiculed him, and yet he allowed it to continue.

"My boy, if you are so smart, tell me why Adonai did not prevent me from acting? If he created me and I am harming his dear children, why did he not make me disappear with a snap of his fingers? His children are constantly calling upon him, praying in all the churches. Why is he not doing anything to bring them back to the divine goodness, which would immediately bring an end to all their suffering? He is strong and powerful, isn't he? Then he just has to remove from the heart of his children the need for power, the need for domination and envy. With that alone, there will be no more wars or oppression. But he is not doing that, and your fable does not make sense!"

Anne was amazed. She knew she was observing a scene that she would probably not be able to report but that was, nevertheless, the most important scene in the life of a person.

Under the dumbfounded gaze of his parents, Nicolas was just like a torch. The answer was already prepared, and his voice struck powerfully. "You know perfectly well the reason for all that. And there is one point about which you don't lie. You are a smart strategist and highly intelligent. God blessed you with this when he created you so that you could educate mankind. And at the time when he revealed himself to a single young family, you decided to rebel. You had the knowledge. You knew that, in the creation, when one element deviates from its original purpose, it is automatically eliminated in order to prevent it from disturbing others and ultimately bringing havoc to the whole. You knew you could not directly attack humanity to destroy it. God would never let you do that. No! You were far more clever than that. When God created man, it was for the purpose of a relation of love, like that between parents and children. You knew that! It is for this reason that man is so different from all other beings of the universe. He is in the image of God, he has within himself all the divine characteristics, and he has the capacity to love like God. He is a creator and thus responsible. My parents would never love me so much if I was a small, obedient robot, programmed like a machine. I am an autonomous being, responsible and free to choose, I am unique. I have in me all that is needed to return an immense love to them, perhaps even greater than the love they give me. It is the key of the universe."

There was a long silence, with not even the slightest sound in the audience. Karl seemed to be dumbfounded. Anne squeezed her husband's arm; he did not react. On Bob's face, a very light smile was floating. Lucifer, devoured by anger, seemed to have lost his voice.

Nicolas coughed to strengthen the voice that apparently had taken over his throat. He made one step further. "You ask me why God did not eliminate you with a snap of his fingers. I shall give you the three reasons for that. First of all, the very process of growth was created by God. Human beings have the duty to pass through certain steps. Their life starts in the mother's womb until they are born in the physical world. From that moment on, their own responsibility is engaged in the process of becoming people who can give and receive pure love. Then, they grow throughout their life in order to become mature, spiritually as well as physically, and be born at last in the spirit world after their physical death. You cannot murder man, but you have deviated him from this noble path. You influenced him like a manipulative teacher and have put in his heart all the ugliness that was in your heart: jealousy, envy, and the drive to dominate and exert power. Carried by your praise and the encouragements you have been whispering in order to justify his deeds, he has been lying, robbing, cheating, oppressing, and slaughtering. But God cannot claim back the free will that he gave to human beings, lest he would make them lower than irresponsible dolls having lost their capacity to be his children. From the beginning, seeing your revolt, God has been warning humanity not to heed you. Men have to make their own way. To deny their responsibility by eliminating you is inconceivable for God because this would amount to denying the whole purpose of his creation and would make it imperfect."

Nicolas's gaze and voice remained steady as he continued. "And secondly, I tell you, don't compare yourself to God. He created you, but your behavior and your fallen deeds do not belong to his divine creation. It is you, and you alone, who have taken on this role of a fallen angel, taking delight in the creation of evil. You have chosen, and your revolt belongs to you alone. If God were to intervene in your behavior, it would mean that your evil deeds are an intrinsic part of his divine creation. But as it is you who is the origin of evil through your own deeds, thinking you—a fallen angel—would become a creator equal to God. God cannot accept that one of his rebellious creatures becomes equal to him. Therefore, he cannot intervene in your behavior."

With confidence and a strength beyond his years, Nicolas presented the third reason. "Finally, you knew that God had created man so that he could inherit the universe. Parents create an environment fit for the well-being of their children. Likewise, God has created such an environment so that, throughout his physical life, man can be happy, can develop, and can become a superior being entitled to be the king of the universe. This he does by taking part in his own creation through perfecting himself in his capacity to love. When this goal is reached, he becomes worthy to rule with love over the universe as God Himself does. How wonderful, isn't it? A world of love and of peace! You had a place as a professor and as a servant in this process, and you left your position. Through your mistake, the current world has nothing to do with what it should have been according to God's initial plan and mankind is still in a state of spiritual immaturity far away from unity with God's parental love. If God had intervened directly and eliminated you right away, it would mean that God gave authority to immature and imperfect men to rule over his creation. In other words, his initial goal would be changed by your mistake. God cannot accept that his creation would end in failure because of you. And these are the three reasons for which he can't destroy you."

Lucifer remained silent as Nicolas concluded his speech. "Everything hinges on human responsibility. From the moment you influence human responsibility, God is blocked. But you can do absolutely nothing if men do not first relate to you. You are the cause of ignorance, obscurantism, and blindness. You and the other fallen angels, you are working to lead mankind away from God. You sow doubts and boast about illuminating human beings through your knowledge, but you spread half-truths and see to it that no one can ever understand this great secret. You should know, however, that all the forces are in motion and that the truth will appear no matter what you do."

Nicolas's speech had been pronounced with a confidence and a power of conviction was beyond understanding. His voice had again changed. If the tone remained the same, the resonance was different. But the impression produced on the participants was unimaginable; they seemed petrified.

Hans looked at Anne with awe. She sought Bob's eyes, but he was like a statue, sitting very straight on his seat and staring straight ahead.

Lucifer raged, "How can you know all that? Who are you?"

"Who talks to you right now? Who is confronting you? I am a twelve-year-old child! You have just revealed to your audience, without even noticing it, the evidence of your powerlessness. Contrary to what you claim, you are not an omniscient God!"

There was a long moment of absolute silence. Nicolas was standing straight up, and he was the image of strength and of righteousness.

Lucifer mumbled incomprehensible words about a trap, set in front of his most faithful disciples. Then his features became distorted with anger, and he screamed.

"Karl! Get rid of Robert. He still belongs to me and is a traitor! You will replace him. Concerning the three others, I have no reason to take them. Kick them out, but don't touch them!"

At that moment, things began moving quickly. The atmosphere became icy. Lucifer's face was covered with black blisters. Like a corpse, he gave off a pestilential odor and then disappeared.

Events then unfolded in an indescribable chaos. Hans held on to Anne, who breathed with difficulty. He took Nicolas in his arms.

At the same time, Bob stood up quickly to take them out the exit, but Karl, more swiftly, took the knife and plunged it into Bob's heart. Bob immediately collapsed, and Hans and Anne were paralyzed by terror.

Karl was transfigured! He turned toward the altar, shook a few drops of blood from the knife on the statue, and chanted, "Beloved Master, O king of kings, I want to be worthy of your trust. Accept this first offering."

The knife still in his hand, he took the vial into the other hand, took off the cap, and spoke again to the statue, "Beloved Master, accept this second offering."

He turned toward Anne and grimaced. "Now you are going to pay!"

When he poured the ashes contained in the vial onto the three candles, a huge fireball burst out. It set ablaze the tablecloth on which the statue was standing. Karl, now a living torch, screamed as his hair and clothes were set on fire. He stumbled, tripped against Bob's body, and fell, dragging the tablecloth and the statue, which rolled onto the ground and shattered into pieces.

A thick smoke immediately spread. People suffocated and screamed. There was no more piety, no more meditation. The gathering was no longer a religious ceremony. Nothing else mattered right now than the frenzy to get out of the blaze and save one's life. The stampede to the exit amongst the screams and insults was daunting.

*

Time goes on.

No one will raise questions about the mysterious opening of the rear door, which had been scrupulously closed during the ceremony.

No one will be able to explain the disappearance of three people attending—a man in his thirties, his wife, and the miraculous child who confronted Lucifer.

No one will have paid attention to the swift and silent man who practically kidnapped them in a silent, black limousine.

No one will be at ease with raising the subject of the frightening closing of this ceremony, neither the foul odor that was emitted, nor the deformed features of Lucifer, nor his sudden disappearance.

On the other hand, all the people attending will remember the threat uttered by Karl and the immediate punishment that struck him down.

Lucifer had said that the woman should not be touched. She and her family were undeniably under some occult protection.

Lucifer had spoken. Karl had transgressed. He paid with his life. The participants will leave this ceremony more demotivated and disunited than ever. And this story will quickly fall into oblivion for people who don't really care about human values.

God knows.

In Seoul, when the murderer had put the ashes of the three dignitaries into a vial, there remained some liquid which, stirred and mixed in this way, had generated a highly flammable product. When the vial came close to the lit candles, it was enough to start the explosion.

Only God knows.

God created the laws of physics.

Chapter 12

On this Friday, December 10, 2010, a mild sun was beaming on Rome. Giovanni Bassoli, alone in the chapel of his monastery, was sitting and praying to God, repenting. Time had weaved its threads since the disappearance of his friend Mahran, but for Giovanni a bond was broken. His mistake had caused Mahran to die. Where had this intuition that Mahran must go to Seoul come from? It is true that his statements, however intuitive they could be, had never gone wrong, and he often saw God's work in them.

But then there was the gas leak and the explosion of the small house in which the meeting had taken place. No one had survived. Giovanni's grief was deep. Mahran still had so many things to accomplish! Mahran was a superior being, and he had sent him to his death.

Ever since the day when the authorities had disclosed the tragedy of Seoul, Giovanni had been unable to accept this reality. He had doubted that the information could be true, expecting his friend to appear one sunny day and tell him that it was a mistake and that he was still alive.

One moment, his eyes were set on a painting upon which the oblique light was falling, there, on the wall facing him. The painting portrayed the first Christian martyr, Stephen, stoned under the watchful gaze of Paul, who, prior to his conversion, was an adamant foe of the Christians. The theological knowledge of Giovanni was vivid. He knew that the sacrifice of Stephen had been instrumental in Paul's living such a strong spiritual experience, that it had transformed the course of his life, making him the greatest Christian missionary.

In this way, the sacrifice of some people allows God to perform miracles, and the greatest miracle ever made to this day had been that of Jesus. Giovanni was a man of God. He followed the footsteps of Jesus, and he was putting Jesus's teaching into practice. He was thus laying a foundation of responsible acts and was drastically rejecting evil. Ah, if all men could be empowered with the same conviction!

Carried by his meditation, he let time pass and was lost in his thoughts, surrounded by the calm of the monastery.

Suddenly, a hand touched his shoulder. He raised his head. "Mahran!"

"Yes, my friend, it is me. I know that you are mourning me. But, you see, I am with you spiritually."

"It is extraordinary! I felt your hand on my shoulder."

"The spiritual matter of which we are made is tangible, and in your case, your spiritual senses are reactivated for a while by the grace of God so that I may convey a message to you."

"I am listening to you."

"You certainly have heard of the book recently written by Anne Standfort?"

"Of course. I read it. It is a highly significant document, and I am happy that it is an international success! But don't tell me that you are connected to this story in one way or another?"

"Do you remember that the voice of the twelve-year-old child who confronted Lucifer was altered several times?"

"I remember that, yes."

"I was one of those voices. God brought us together—the Jewish chief rabbi, the Muslim grand mufti, and me—to give us the mission to confront Lucifer through the child. And the message of God is vibrant in us. Religions, all of them, should come together, support one another, and fight together against our common enemy, Lucifer."

"Your sacrifice was not in vain, then. I suppose that it contributed to the conversion of the wealthy figure who was killed at the end of the ceremony?"

"Absolutely. Our unconditional sacrifice allowed God to convert this old man. The inspiration then came to him to have this book written, and he carefully sought the most suitable person. He found Anne Standfort. The strength of this woman and the trust she placed in him led her to take part in this ceremony. It was the necessary outcome so that Lucifer revealed his true nature in front of his most faithful disciples. God's will, once again, was done."

A light fog began fading. Mahran was gone.

Giovanni was now smiling. He took a few steps forward, looked again at the painting, and whispered, almost to himself, "So, then, it was all an amazing divine trap!"

Epilogue

October 31, 2024

The book was published as scheduled. As expected, it was a complete success. As expected, it was criticized, and yet it sold well. Following Bob's instructions, the profits are regularly placed into Anne's account, to be used for a new edition. The book can be found in libraries but not yet in universities. One day, maybe?

Hans, Anne, and Nicolas never returned to Basel. Someone took care of emptying their apartment. Their furniture and personal belongings were carried away to a beautiful region of forests and valleys, where an English-style cottage was purchased in their name and carefully decorated.

They now have a pretty nice piece of land, and Hans, who proved to have a talent for gardening, is actively cultivating it. They also take care of a few hens and rabbits. From his talents as a banker, he has kept only his sense of regularity. The earth and the animals also need to be cared for regularly.

Anne is writing for a women's magazine, and she gives communication lessons for adults. People like to consult her when they meet difficulties in relationships. They say she helps them become gentle.

They left the concrete for the tillable earth, the neon lights for the color of the sky. In their small home there is music, birds sing, and there is no television.

The money left over from the expenses for publishing and distributing the book has been wisely used. In one place children needed care. In another, a school was needed. Somewhere else, water had to be found. Anne and Hans have made good decisions. They have enough income, have few needs, and are busy living a simple life.

Nicolas completed high school and then studied botanical science. His special powers remained an enigma, dormant. Would they re-surface one day? He didn't seem much concerned about it. He is now a forest warden in the region and lives, with his wife, two miles from his parents. He is a handsome man, strong and peaceful, who looks at the world with lucidity and benevolence.

Each year, toward the end of October, they have a visit from a friend whose very black hair has much whitened. He has announced his visit for today—and, of course, the table is set.

Pascal Roussel

Made in the USA
Middletown, DE
28 April 2017